'I don't think I know the happened...

'...of why my mother left. I feel as though I'm stuck in some other dimension, as though my life's on hold.' Hannah's voice trembled with emotion.

Adam drew her close to him, and she registered the warmth of his embrace just as if he had folded a warm blanket around her, sheltering her from a cold, harsh wind.

'I wish I could take some of the hurt away from you,' he murmured, his voice softening, his grey gaze moving over her with slow deliberation, smoothing over her like a balm to her shattered senses.

He leaned towards her, his long body gently pressuring hers, urging her to nestle up against him. She could feel the steady beat of his heart beneath her cheek, and she lifted her gaze to him. Then slowly, compellingly, his head lowered and his mouth claimed the softness of her lips.

When **Joanna Neil** discovered Mills & Boon®, her life-long addiction to reading crystallised into an exciting new career writing Medical Romance™. Her characters are probably the outcome of her varied lifestyle, which includes working as a clerk, typist, nurse and infant teacher. She enjoys dressmaking and cooking at her Leicestershire home. Her family includes a husband, son and daughter, an exuberant yellow Labrador and two slightly crazed cockatiels. She currently works with a team of tutors at her local education centre to provide creative writing workshops for people interested in exploring their own writing ambitions.

Recent titles by the same author:

IN HIS TENDER CARE
THE CONSULTANT'S SPECIAL RESCUE
THE EMERGENCY DOCTOR'S PROPOSAL
HER BOSS AND PROTECTOR

THE LONDON DOCTOR

BY

JOANNA NEIL

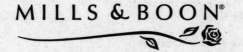

MILLS & BOON®

First published in Great Britain 2006
Harlequin Mills & Boon Limited,
Eton House, 18-24 Paradise Road, Richmond, Surrey TW9 1SR

© Joanna Neil 2006

ISBN 0 263 84743 8

Set in Times Roman 10½ on 12¾ pt
03-0706-47894

Printed and bound in Spain
by Litografia Rosés, S.A., Barcelona

CHAPTER ONE

HANNAH pulled the door of her flat firmly shut. It wasn't a good fit against the frame, and she made a face, struggling with the lock, but she wasn't going to let it deter her from making certain that everything was secure. There wasn't all that much to recommend the accommodation, but at least it was a place to stay while she was going to be working in London for the next few months.

'Is you going out?' a small voice piped up from the bottom of the stairs, and Hannah glanced to where the sound was coming from.

'Hello, Ellie,' she said, peering down to see the little girl from the ground-floor flat. 'Yes, I'm on my way to work at the hospital. Are you waiting to go off to nursery school?' Hannah started down the stairs, her mouth curving as she came closer to the child.

The three-year-old was sitting on the bottom step, cuddling a soft toy to her chest, but now she twisted around and looked up at Hannah once more. She nodded solemnly, her bright golden curls quivering. 'We was s'posed to be going ages ago, but Mummy's late. She couldn't get up this morning. She sleeped and sleeped and I had to keep nudging her.'

'She's awake now, though, isn't she?' Hannah frowned momentarily. After the disturbed night they had just gone through, she wasn't really surprised that Ellie's mother wasn't firing on all cylinders this morning, but at least Ellie had slept through everything.

It had taken Hannah all that she had to get herself ready for work this morning, but this was her first day in a new job and she was determined to be there in good time. It didn't bode too well that she was feeling drained of energy before she even started, though.

Ellie nodded, dancing the teddy bear on her knees. 'She forgetted something. She's gone back to get it.'

Hannah came to the last step and sat down beside the little girl. 'He's a lovely teddy bear, isn't he?' she murmured, lightly stroking the silky fur. 'What's his name?'

Ellie's gaze met hers in an unwavering blue stare. 'His name's Teddy,' she said.

'Oh, well, yes, of course, it would be, wouldn't it?' Hannah chuckled softly. 'Is he going to nursery school with you?'

'Yes.' Ellie looked surprised. 'He goes everywhere with me.'

Just then Ellie's mother emerged from her flat, looking harassed. 'Hi, Hannah,' she said, throwing her a quick, friendly glance. She had the same blue eyes as her daughter, but she was a brunette, her hair glossy and shoulder length, pinned back with two gold clips. 'We're running late today. All that upheaval with Dean upstairs meant that it took me ages to get to sleep afterwards. I kept worrying about what might have happened if we hadn't gone in and helped out.'

'It was a good thing that his smoke alarm was working,' Hannah agreed, 'otherwise things might have been much worse. He's obviously having trouble getting about since his knee operation, and we all had a lucky escape. I dread to think what might have happened—the chip-pan fire could have set light to the whole building if we hadn't gone in when we did.'

'Do you think he'll be all right?' Abby asked. 'He's seemed depressed lately and I can't help feeling that we ought to do something to help out. I have to go to the office this morning, though, so he'll be on his own here.'

'I'm not sure what more we can do, just at the moment. He was half-asleep when I went to look in on him this morning, but he said that his knee was troubling him and that he was going to take some painkillers and go back to bed for a while. He's supposed to be going for a check-up at the hospital later on today—around two o'clock, he said.'

'I'll be home by then. I'll have a word with him at lunchtime, and make sure that he's up and about. He'll need a hand with cleaning up some of the smoke damage, anyway.'

'Thanks, Abby. I'll feel better knowing that we're both going to keep an eye on him from now on.' It shouldn't be too difficult to do that—Dean's flat occupied half of the second floor, opposite Hannah's, while Abby and her daughter had a two-bedroomed flat taking up the whole of the ground floor.

Abby glanced at her watch. 'I must go—I have to drop Ellie off at nursery school before I go in to work.'

'Me, too... I want to get in to work early so that I can familiarise myself with everything before I have to make a start.'

Hannah said her goodbyes and left the house, hurriedly making her way to the tube station. With any luck, her journey would only take around half an hour and then she would have just a two-minute walk to the City Hospital. Once there, she was hoping to have time to find her bearings and adjust herself to her new role as senior house officer in A and E.

She wasn't sure what to expect. Everyone had said that this was the best teaching hospital around, and she was lucky to have landed a post here, even though it was only for a six-month stretch. Her nerves were already beginning to get the better of her, though, and when she finally arrived at her destination, the hospital seemed to loom up in front of her. It was an imposing building. It was a huge, sprawling, impersonal place, like the city, and she faltered, wondering whether she might have made a mistake in coming here.

After a moment, she went inside. At least she had made friends with her neighbours, the people who shared the house with her. Getting to know Abby and her daughter had been good. It went part way to making the cramped living conditions seem more bearable. Dean, the young man who lived in the flat across the hallway from Hannah, was a bit of an unknown quantity as yet, but he seemed sociable enough.

'So, you're the new SHO?' Mr Tremayne, the consultant, was a tall man, in his mid-forties, she guessed, and he had black hair, silvering a little around the edges, giving him a distinguished look.

She nodded, and he said, 'Good. Grab yourself some protective covering and you can help out over here. We've had an influx of patients from a road traffic accident, and we need every pair of hands we can get hold of.'

He was clearly not going to waste any time on preliminaries. 'I was going to put you with our specialist registrar, but he has his hands full right now, and Colin could do with some help in the meantime. He's trying to save a man's leg. Compound shaft of femur fracture—as well as tibial fracture. The circulation could be compromised. When you've finished there, you can go and look for our registrar.'

He paused, then threw back, almost as an afterthought, 'He's from the same neck of the woods as you, I believe—the Chilterns, isn't it? Even the same area, I think.'

Hannah was puzzled. It sounded as though he thought she might know the man, but she didn't know anyone who worked in London. As it was, she was more than a little distracted by being thrown in at the deep end. She didn't have time right now to worry about who the specialist registrar might be.

No matter how edgy she might be feeling, Colin, the doctor she had temporarily been assigned to, appeared to be even more so. He looked worried. His dark hair fell in a haphazard way across his brow, giving him a youthful look.

'The analgesia isn't adequate,' he said, assessing his

patient who was groaning and clearly suffering. 'I'm going to have to try a femoral nerve block.' He glanced at the nurse who was assisting. 'Sarah, have you had any luck finding the orthopaedic surgeon yet?'

'He's on his way.'

He sent Hannah a quick look. 'Check the dosage of lignocaine with me, will you? He's going to need the maximum.'

Hannah did as she was asked, then cleaned the patient's skin in preparation for the insertion of the needle. Colin started the procedure, inserting the needle perpendicular to the skin and lateral to the artery, then aspirated and checked for blood, before starting to inject the local anaesthetic. He moved the needle, fanning it in and out laterally. After a moment, he sucked in his breath and, though he didn't say anything, Hannah guessed that he had punctured the artery.

'I'll have to start again, as soon as the bleeding stops,' he muttered. He apologised to his patient, who screwed up his eyes and clenched his hands.

'Do you want me to compress the area?' Hannah asked. It wasn't his fault. It happened sometimes, and she felt sorry for both Colin and the patient.

He nodded. 'Give it five minutes, and then I'll try again. I'll take a wound swab while we're waiting. We're giving him cefuroxime in case of infection, but I may need to add metronidazole.'

The next time, when he tried the nerve block, he was successful. Hannah hurried to prepare the backslab in order to immobilise the limb and Colin covered the wound with povidone-iodine soaks.

'That should hold things until he goes for surgery,' he said. He sent Hannah a quick look. 'You've not come to us on the best of days. It feels as though all hell's been let loose round here.'

'So it seems.' She gave a weak smile. 'I was supposed to be working with the specialist registrar when I've finished helping you—do you know where he is?'

'He was with a patient in cubicle three last time I saw him, but he could be anywhere by now. Adam's one of those quicksilver figures—you never know with him. He might be working on a cardiac patient, or he could be supervising a student. It always seems as though he's in three places at once.'

'I saw him going over to the coffee machine a while back,' Sarah put in. She was a pretty young woman, a brunette, with grey eyes that reflected an outgoing personality. She waved a hand in the direction of a bay that was set back from the main area of A and E. 'You can grab something to drink from there any time you like, while you're on the move, in between breaks.'

'Thanks. That's useful to know.'

She sent Hannah a querying look. 'I heard you were from somewhere around the West Wycombe area. Perhaps you know Adam already? His father's Monroe Driscoll—you know, the Driscoll import-export conglomerate? He has a big country estate round about where you come from. Perhaps you've seen it?'

Hannah felt a prickling sensation run down the back of her neck. 'Yes, I know the estate.' Her voice sounded hollow in her ears.

Sarah was looking at a point beyond her. 'Adam,' she said, 'we were just talking about you.' She directed a hand towards Hannah. 'This is Hannah, our new SHO. Perhaps you two already know each other?'

Hannah half turned as the specialist registrar approached. She looked him over, her gaze transfixed. Adam Driscoll was every bit the man she remembered…long and lean, rangy and confident in his stride, his features perfectly sculpted, his hair as black as jet. Her heart tripped into a thudding, erratic beat in response to his nearness, and it bothered her that he still had the power to enthral her, to make her go weak at the knees.

She stared at him and all the memories came flooding back in full force. Their last meeting had not been a happy one. Harsh words had been said, and recriminations left to hang in the air. The same brooding tension rose up between them now as though the years had dropped away in an instant.

Adam's gaze travelled over her steadily, with cool intent. 'Oh, yes,' he said. 'We've met before, haven't we, Hannah?'

He said it with a wry inflection, his deep voice gritty, his grey eyes dark and glittering, giving nothing away, but he remembered, just as she did, she was sure of it.

He flicked a glance towards Sarah and Colin. 'In fact, we've known each other since Hannah was in her teens and came to live in the village. At one time, she and her foster-brother were frequent visitors to my father's estate…in fact, they even worked there sometimes in the summer holidays.'

'Oh, that must have been something special,' Sarah murmured. 'I've seen the place in the brochures. It looks lovely, set in all that sprawling, beautiful countryside.'

Hannah's mouth made an awkward twist. 'Yes, you're right. It's just as wonderful as it looks from the photographs.'

Adam said calmly, 'Perhaps we should find a quiet corner where we can go and talk. I need to show you around the department and fill you in on how we organise things here.'

He turned and she went after him, her steps trailing, almost reluctant, yet drawn to follow him as though by some magnetic impulse. Hadn't it always been that way? As a young girl, she had been mesmerised by him, had needed him, wanted him, but in the end all her dreams had turned to ashes.

'It must be all of five or six years,' he said, opening the door to an office and going in there, pausing to glance down at a file on the desk. 'Even longer, perhaps, since we last saw each other.'

He was probably right. Although he had come back to his family estate since then, on fleeting visits during breaks from his work, she had always been careful to keep away, after that last bitter parting.

Adam pushed the file to one side and cleared a space, half leaning, half sitting on the edge of the table, facing her, his long legs thrust out in front of him. 'I suppose you were busy with your medical training in all that time…at a medical school close to where your adoptive mother lived, wasn't it? And various other places since, I imagine. I didn't think you would ever stray this far afield—not to London, at least. Cities aren't really your style, are they? You're a country girl at heart.'

'Is there something wrong with that?' Her blue eyes challenged him.

He shook his head. 'Nothing at all. It just surprises me to see you here, away from your home territory.'

'I heard that this was the best teaching hospital around. It was an opportunity I couldn't miss.'

'Maybe.' He looked at her thoughtfully, and she could see that he wasn't convinced. He was too perceptive by far, and it made her deeply uncomfortable to know that he might guess what was her driving force. She wasn't ready to share her true reason for coming here with anyone, yet. Her self-confidence was too fragile, too easily shattered, and she was afraid that if she admitted too much, everything would fall through.

He frowned. 'So, how's your foster-brother these days? Is he managing to stay out of trouble?'

'You don't think that's possible, do you?' It was her turn to study him, her gaze clear and direct. He had brought up the source of their hostility towards one another, and she wasn't going to back down from that. 'He wasn't guilty of any wrongdoing, but your father wouldn't listen to reason, would he? Ryan didn't take that money. He isn't a thief. You all blamed him, and treated him despicably, but he was innocent.'

Adam shrugged. 'That's all water under the bridge now, isn't it? We've all moved on from there.'

'Have we? How can we move on when those things are still unsettled? Those accusations were hurtful, and the sting lingers on, even years after the event.'

'Hasn't your brother moved on? I thought he might have become less restless over the years…that he might be less easily roused to anger. He was always quick-tempered and ready to fly off the handle at the slightest provocation. You can hardly blame my father if he had his doubts about him. There was gossip. People talked and they always had something to say about the kids from Calder Close.'

Hannah glowered at him. 'And that was always the gospel truth, was it? We were all part of a foster-family, and children came and went, and we had no solid foundation—that meant we were bound to be up to no good, did it? What was it that made us a target—that we were all misfits from a bad gene pool?'

'I didn't say that.' His jaw tightened. 'I'm just pointing out that people had their doubts, and Ryan didn't do anything to convince them otherwise.' His glance flicked over her, taking in her slender figure, coming to linger on the mass of her shimmering, honey-gold curls, but she had no way of knowing what he was thinking. The air sparked between them. 'Anyway, you and your foster-brother didn't come and go, like the other children, did you? You stayed. You, for one, were adopted and you didn't go back to your parents.'

Her gaze faltered. It hurt to remember those childhood years. 'Ryan did, from time to time. His parents managed to unscramble themselves on occasion, as I recall, but he was happy with our foster-mum. She gave him stability of sorts.'

'That's true, I suppose.' An ambulance siren sounded in the distance and he got to his feet in one fluid movement. 'We should get back to work. There might just be time for me to show you around before we get caught up in the melee once more.'

He left her to meet up with the paramedics a few minutes later, and she worked steadily through the rest of the morning, trying to keep her mind firmly on the job in hand. It had been a shock, meeting up with him like this, and she wasn't at all sure what was the best way to handle the situation. It looked as though he was going to be supervising her work for a good deal of the time, and things were by no means settled between them. Perhaps they never would be.

His father had dismissed Ryan from his job on the estate, and that knowledge still rankled. No one had actually ever labelled Ryan a thief, but the implication had been there, and her foster-brother had never come to terms with that. It had hurt him to be branded a ne'er-do-well, and Hannah recognised that and had been fiercely loyal to him to the last.

He wasn't a blood relation to her, but they had been brought up together for a good many years, and she treated him as though he was her brother. Adam's part in the whole sorry episode had unsettled her and had destroyed their tenuous relationship. He had sided with his father, and Hannah felt bad about that.

Colin came and found her after the lunch break. 'How are you holding up?' he asked. 'You look as though you're a bit out of your depth. Can I help at all?'

'Thanks. I might need propping up before too long.' Her mouth made an odd quirk. 'Everything's so imme-diate, and there's hardly a moment where you can stop and think. I still haven't quite found my bearings. The whole place is like a warren, and I've lost my way on more than one occasion.'

She grimaced, recalling how Adam had sharply intervened when she had nearly taken a patient down to the basement instead of up to Theatre, and she was still smarting from his cool admonition when she had been about to start treatment on a patient before waiting for lab results to come back. It had appeared to her to be totally necessary, but how could she have known that the man was a drug user who was known to the department for his wily subterfuges?

She hurried over to the paramedics as they brought in another patient. The man on the trolley was semiconscious, with an oxygen mask over his face, and Hannah gave him a cursory glance, anxious to examine him and find out what needed to be done. She could see that his breathing was shallow and barely perceptible. He was slipping deeper into oblivion.

'What happened to him?' she asked.

'It looks like a co-proxamol overdose,' the paramedic said. 'There was a bottle of tablets on his bedside table and, judging by the date they were prescribed, there are a lot missing. His neighbour found him.'

'OK, thanks.' Hannah supervised the patient's transfer to a cubicle, and prepared to intubate him, but as she removed the mask from his face, she drew back in sudden alarm. 'I know this man,' she said, throwing Sarah a quick glance. 'He lives in the flat opposite mine.'

Dean looked in a bad way, and she had to quickly

overcome the jolt to her system to make sure that she did whatever was possible to save him.

'I'm going to put in an intravenous line and give him naxolone to try to reverse any cardiorespiratory effects,' she told Sarah. 'I'll add N-acetylcysteine in dextrose as well, but we'll need to check the prothrombin time and repeat the infusion accordingly.'

'Are you going to do a gastric lavage?' Sarah asked.

Hannah nodded. 'Yes, I'm going to put in a nasogastric tube. Let's get him into a head-down position, and I'll need two litres of warm water.'

Inside, Hannah was feeling shaky. She ought to have known that something was wrong when she had spoken to Dean this morning. If anything happened to him, she would feel responsible. Guilt washed over her. She had to save him...she had to...

She glanced up as her friend Abby appeared in the doorway. She looked fraught, concerned, as though she was in shock.

'They said he was in here,' Abby managed. 'Is it all right if I stay? I need to know that he's going to be all right. I had to get the landlord to come and open his door so that we could get in, and it took ages. I felt sure that something was wrong.'

'Yes, of course you can stay,' Hannah said. 'It won't be pleasant, though. You might want to look away. As soon as I've washed out his stomach, I'm going to give him charcoal to prevent any more absorption of the drug he's taken.'

'Is it very dangerous, what he's taken?' Abby asked. 'I mean, how bad is it?'

'The drug contains paracetamol,' Hannah explained as she worked. 'It can cause irreparable liver damage, or even liver failure, if the overdose is large enough and we don't clear it from his system.'

She turned to Sarah and said anxiously, 'I need to find out why he took so many tablets.'

'Should we get a psychiatric consultation?'

'Possibly. I'll wait until I know more.' She glanced at Abby. 'Do we know if there are any relatives we should contact?'

Abby grimaced. 'I'm not sure. He said something to me about his parents—I think they live somewhere in Kent. I'll see if I can find out exactly where.'

'Thanks. I think that would be a good idea.'

Abby stayed for a while, but she was increasingly restless, and after an hour had passed, she looked at her watch and said, 'I can't wait any longer. I have to go and fetch Ellie from nursery school or she'll wonder where I am.' She bit her lip. 'There's been no change in his condition, has there? Is he going to get through this?'

Hannah glanced at her. 'We're doing everything we can, Abby, but it could take several hours before we can say for certain that he's out of danger. I'll let you know what's happening, I promise.'

'Thanks.' Abby left, looking worried, and after a minute or two, Adam put his head round the door.

'You're still keeping watch over him, I see. Perhaps you should take a break, and then go and see to some of your other patients. There are a lot of people out there who need your attention, and the queue is getting longer by the minute.'

She looked at him, her face pale. 'But I know him. He lives in the same building as me, and I have to see him through this.'

'You're doing everything that you can. When Sarah comes back from suturing her patient, she'll observe him and let you know if there's any change.'

He was right, of course, but it tore her to pieces to leave Dean like this. She said anxiously, 'Are you sure there's nothing more that I can do for him? I've been trying to think of alternatives that I might have missed.'

He glanced at Dean's chart. 'It looks as though you may have found out why he took so many painkillers. He has an infected wound on his knee…is that right?'

She nodded. 'Yes, he does. He had an operation recently to repair the ligament, and somehow it became infected. I've taken a swab for the lab and I'm giving him antibiotic cover in the meantime.'

'Then you've done enough for now. When you get the results back from the lab you'll be able to choose a more specific treatment.'

She didn't have any more arguments to put forward, and there was no denying he was right when he said that she had other patients to attend to. Reluctantly, she followed Adam out of the cubicle as Sarah came back to check Dean's blood pressure and pulse.

'You know, you're going to have to find a way of distancing yourself from your patients,' Adam said. 'If you get too deeply involved with them like this, you'll be nothing but a shadow of yourself by the time you finish your stint here. You can't afford to expend all that emotional energy.'

'I don't suppose you ever let that happen to you, do you?' she remarked flatly. 'You make it sound as though it's easy to let go.'

'I realise that it must be hard for you, but it's something we all have to learn. Emotionally, we're all vulnerable and you have to find a way to keep part of yourself detached, or you simply won't be able to do your job.'

'And you manage yours perfectly, don't you?' Her gaze challenged him. 'You don't let things bother you. You don't worry about what happens afterwards, when the damage has been done. You simply let go and you move on as though it's none of your concern.'

Wasn't that what he had done when Ryan had been in trouble? It had hurt all the more because she had idolised Adam, worshipped him from afar, compelled by his strength and firm character, and it had been as though he had let her down when she'd most needed his support.

He frowned. 'This isn't a little cottage hospital where you get to know your patients and probably even live near them. This is the city, and our intake runs into the thousands. You can't afford to let yourself care so much about everyone who comes through here.'

She lifted her head, her mouth straightening. 'No, I suppose you can't. That wouldn't do at all, would it?'

His gaze ran over her. 'I said that you don't belong in the city, and it's true, isn't it? I'm not sure that you're anywhere near tough enough to stand the pace—and it will overwhelm you, unless you manage to build up your confidence somehow, so that you're better able to cope with everything that comes your way.' He grimaced.

'Perhaps you'd have done better to stay in the country-side, where you could work in a close-knit, rural community.'

She looked into his eyes. 'But I'm here now, and I plan to stay. I'm sorry if that doesn't fit in with your plans.'

He watched her, his expression cloaked, but she moved away from him and went in search of her next patient. No matter what he said, or thought, she wasn't going to back down. She was here for a special reason…she was here to find her natural mother, and there was no going back. It was something she needed to do. If he didn't like it that she was here, that was too bad.

Hannah just didn't know, right now, how exactly she was going to cope, working alongside him day after day. Once she had held a torch for him, and the flame had burned brightly, fiercely, until a cold, harsh wind had blown it out. Now their differences were too deeply ingrained for things to be easily resolved.

CHAPTER TWO

'DID you manage to get in touch with Dean's parents?' Hannah asked, glancing across her tiny kitchen to where Abby was standing in the doorway. She added water to the coffee machine and set the jug on its base to heat up.

Abby nodded. 'Sort of. I found their phone number, but they were out when I called, so I left a message, telling them what had happened. I gave them my number in case they wanted to get in touch.' She frowned. 'Do you think Dean will come through this all right?'

'I hope so. It was a good thing that you looked in on him at lunchtime, or things might have been much worse for him. As it was, in the end we admitted him so that we could go on with his treatment, and his medical team will work to try to clear up the problems with his knee. They were taking him up to one of the wards as I came off duty and he seemed to have roused a little by then.'

She didn't tell Abby that there was still the danger of a relapse. She didn't want to upset her friend, but in these situations there were sometimes ongoing problems, depending on the action of the drug that had been taken.

'I'm just glad that Ellie was at nursery school—it would have been really upsetting for her to see him in that state.' Abby glanced behind her, looking through to the living room where Ellie was playing with her dolls.

Hannah nodded and poured coffee into two mugs, setting them out on a tray with cream and sugar. 'We could take these through to the living room,' she suggested. 'There's hardly room to move in here.' She sent a brief glance around the room, taking in the single drainer sink, the cooker and the fridge. There was nothing more. It was what, in estate agent's terms, they called cosy or compact…which meant that there was barely room in there for her, let alone enough space for two people to stand about, chatting.

The living room was bigger, but the furnishings were sparse—there was a settee, a table and chairs, and her bed. Perhaps she would buy a decorative screen to hide that part of the room and set it apart from the rest.

What would Adam make of her poky flat if he were ever to see it? She didn't know where he was living in London, but it was close to the hospital, from what she had heard, and his accommodation was more than likely something special. His father's house was a mansion, compared to this, and she guessed he was used to the best.

Occasionally, she had been to events held in the extensive gardens on the family estate, and Adam had shown her around on her seventeenth birthday, giving her the full tour. She had been overwhelmed by the splendour of it.

They went and sat with Ellie, watching her play as they sipped their coffee. The little girl was totally absorbed in her game, her face intent and purposeful as she wiped her doll's cheeks with a paper towel and then combed her hair. Watching her, Hannah smiled, before turning her attention to Abby once more.

'Do you see much of your parents?' she asked.

Abby shook her head. 'We didn't get on,' she said. 'There were lots of arguments, and then things finally came to a head when they didn't approve of my boy-friend—Ellie's father. I was young and headstrong, and deeply in love, and I followed him to London, despite their protests. In the end they were right, though. He didn't have any staying power—he wasn't the man that I thought he was.' Her expression was sad, and Hannah felt uncomfortable that she had brought the subject up in the first place.

'I'm sorry,' she murmured. 'I didn't mean to rake up bad memories.' She sent Abby a swift glance. 'Is there any chance that you will make things up with them?'

'I don't think so. I waited a while, and then I started to send them cards and letters from time to time, but they didn't get in touch, so I've let it go. I thought they might want to get to know Ellie, but obviously I was wrong.' She made a face. 'I sometimes think Ellie's missing out on so much—her grandparents, and family life, and all the green open spaces where I used to live. There's no garden here for her, and I feel that I'm letting her down.'

Hannah didn't know what to say. There was no way that things could be put right in a short space of time, and Abby was clearly still troubled by the long-standing estrangement from her parents.

She said, 'Perhaps what we all need is a break, a chance to get away from being cramped up in these flats. Maybe we could arrange an afternoon out some time. We could have a picnic in the park, or we might try a boat trip along the Thames.'

Abby brightened. 'A boat trip would be lovely. I'm sure Ellie would enjoy that.'

'That's what we'll do, then. I'll try and sort something out for next weekend, if you like—unfortunately, I have to work tomorrow and Sunday.'

'That would be great. It will give us something to look forward to.'

Hannah remembered their conversation on Sunday morning, when she was travelling on the tube on her way to work. It would do them all good to have some time out. She found herself longing for the green fields and the beech woods and the sleepy village she had left behind when she had come to work in London. Most of all, she missed her adoptive mother and father.

There was no time to dwell on these things, though. As soon as she arrived at the hospital, she went to check on Dean, and discovered that he was at least responding to the medication. He wasn't talkative, but he looked in better shape than he had been yesterday or the day before.

Things were chaotic when she walked into A and E, and she was plunged straight into work. Mr Tremayne was nowhere to be seen, and Adam was the senior man in his place, the one who decided on who did what and when.

'I think I prefer it when Adam's in charge,' Sarah commented, grabbing supplies from the storeroom. 'You know where you are with him. He's efficient and confident, and you can rely on him. He always seems to know what to do, and he never dithers or mulls things over for too long when you need an instant answer.'

Hannah was more guarded in her reaction to him. Her feelings were too raw where he was concerned, but she found herself watching him compulsively. Today, he was wearing a beautifully tailored grey suit, and there was no denying he looked good. His hair gleamed under the overhead lights, and he had that mark of authority, tempered with compassion towards his patients.

He was decisive, but thorough, and he seemed to thrive on the constant rush of adrenaline, whereas it had the opposite effect on her. She wilted at the mere prospect of instigating life-changing procedures. She sometimes wondered whether she was cut out for work in A and E.

'There's a patient in cubicle two who is waiting to be seen,' Adam said. 'I want you to take a look at her. She's complaining of abdominal pain, and she's been vomiting. We've had one or two people in this morning suffering from food poisoning, so you should look out for that, and check whether she's had any food from the same source as the others. We'll need to liaise with environmental health if she has.'

He didn't acknowledge her in any other way, and part of her was glad of that. She was far too conscious of him as it was, and it was going to be difficult enough working with Adam over the next few months, with their past history getting in the way.

She tended to the patient in cubicle two and then spent the next couple of hours dealing with a wide variety of cases that challenged her abilities at every turn.

When Adam caught up with her, he asked briskly, 'What happened with your abdominal patient?' He glanced at his chart. 'It says here that you've put her on IV fluids and sent her up to Theatre.'

'There was a degree of tenderness in the right iliac fossa, and her history suggested appendicitis.' She looked at him, expecting trouble, but he simply nodded and moved on.

Hannah stared after him. She had been ready to argue her case, but he hadn't said another word about it, and now she was flummoxed. It was impossible to know what to make of him.

Just then, though, Sarah called her over to the phone, and she put all thoughts of him out of her mind.

'It's your mother,' Sarah said. 'She was going to ring off, rather than disturb you, but I told her that you were free to talk.'

'Thanks.' Hannah took the receiver from Sarah, and heard her adoptive mother's voice. 'Hello, Mum,' she said. 'Is everything all right?'

'It's fine. I didn't really want to call you at work,' her mother said hurriedly. 'It's just that it's Sunday, and you haven't been at home when I've called lately. I want to know how you are getting on. Is it all working out all right for you?'

Hannah felt a warm surge of affection for this woman who had taken the place of her mother and had cared for her since the age of ten. The bond between them was a strong one, and Hannah had been accepted into her home from the first as if she had been her own daughter.

'I tried to ring you,' Hannah said, 'but we somehow kept missing each other. Yes, I think it's working out all right for me. It's been quite hectic, but I'm beginning to get the hang of things. It isn't like ordinary medicine, working in A and E. Sometimes, I hardly have time to stop and think.'

'How are you taking to life in the city? Is it what you expected?' Her mother sounded doubtful.

'It's exactly as I thought it would be,' Hannah admitted. 'I'm still having trouble finding my way around but, then, I haven't had much time to explore my surroundings. I think it will be all right in time. There's a lot I want to see.'

They spoke for a while longer, and when Hannah put down the receiver, a wave of homesickness swept over her. She was overcome by a sudden feeling of being lost and alone, adrift at sea.

'Is there a problem?' Adam asked. 'Was that your mother that you were talking to just now? I thought I heard you mention her name.'

Hannah gave a small start. She hadn't even realised that he was close by, and now she looked at him warily. Was he going to tell her that she should be getting on with her work?

'Yes, it was my mum, but there's no problem,' she

murmured. 'I was just about to go and find my next patient.'

He looked at her steadily, his grey eyes searching her face. 'You looked vulnerable and unsure of yourself. I haven't seen you look like that since you were a young girl and your mother brought you that first time to buy apples from the orchards on my father's estate.' He made a wry face. 'As I recall, back then you were a skinny kid with big, bewildered eyes and a scared-rabbit stare. You looked wary and unsettled, as though you were about to take your heels and run.'

'Perhaps I was.' She sent him a fleeting glance. 'We had just moved house. I was confused, and insecure. There had been so many changes in my life, and here I was, moving to a new area with my foster-parents. I wasn't sure that this latest home would be any different to the others. They told me they wanted to adopt me, but I didn't really expect it to happen or believe that I would be staying there for long.'

He nodded. 'Things haven't altered much since then, have they? You still have that haunted look about you, as though you're looking for an escape route.'

'Do I?' Was he intent on provoking her? He had been so insistent that she didn't belong here, and it seemed as though in a way he was still trying to prove his point. She gave a faint shrug. 'I can't complain. My mum was good to me—she's still good to me, and I love her dearly.'

'I never really understood the fostering bit…why it should go on for such a long time. After all, you hadn't had any contact with your natural mother—not for ages at any rate. I'd have expected that you would have been adopted earlier. That might have provided you with a stronger feeling of security.'

'Maybe, but, as far as I know, my real mother wouldn't agree to it at first. I'm not sure why. I don't remember much about her now, except that she flitted in and out of my life when I was a young child. Perhaps subconsciously I've chosen to forget. I think she was very young when she became pregnant with me, and perhaps she found that she couldn't cope. I know that she had a nervous breakdown when I was very young, and then she was ill again when I was about ten or eleven years old. That's more or less when they started to talk about adoption.'

'You sound as though you're beginning to try to understand her and possibly even starting to feel sorry for her.' Adam's gaze flicked over her tense features. 'I wouldn't have thought you owed her any loyalty.'

'Perhaps you're right.' She looked away. It made her feel awkward and uneasy, talking about her real mother. Her memories, such as they were, were filled with a mixture of sadness and uncertainty. Whenever she had thought that at last she could relax and feel safe, her mother would disappear again. It had been bewildering to a young child, and even now she couldn't make any sense of it.

That was why she needed finally to seek her out, and it was the reason for her coming to London. She had begun to feel as though she was in limbo, in that indeterminate state where she was unable to move ahead and get on with her life. She had reached the stage where she desperately wanted answers to questions that had been left over from her childhood.

'Didn't you ever have any contact with your father? I know you spoke about him once or twice, but I don't remember you ever going to stay with him,' Adam said.

'I don't think he wanted much contact with me. He married my mother, but I think he only did that because he felt that it was the right thing to do. In fact, I think he was completely taken aback when he discovered that she was expecting his child. I know that he was ambitious, and his work must have been more important to him than anything else because he felt as though he was held back by the marriage and it didn't last long. I do remember my mother saying that he went off to follow his career.'

She glanced at him. 'I expect you would understand all about that—the work bit, I mean—feeling the need to achieve more and more.' Hadn't he always been ambitious and career orientated?

His eyes narrowed. 'Is there something wrong with that?'

'I suppose not.' She grimaced. 'Anyway, I don't recall very much more about him. He was always a shadowy figure, as far as I was concerned, and I never really had the chance to get to know him better. I never will. He died some years ago.'

He might have said something in response, but Mr Tremayne walked into the department just then, a harassed look on his face. 'We've had an alert from the ambulance service,' he said. 'We need to start following major incident procedure, and I'm going to set up a control centre here.'

He looked at Adam. 'We need to prepare the department so that we can receive patients from the incident area. I want you to give out action cards to all the staff, and make sure that they have labels to denote who is who. I'm going to prepare a triage point at the ambulance entrance.'

Adam nodded. 'I'll make sure that the theatres are on standby, and I'll clear X-ray and the scanner ready for the influx.'

'That's good.' Mr Tremayne drew Adam to one side and spoke to him for a few minutes longer and then went on his way to assemble the rest of the staff.

'What's happened?' Hannah asked. 'What kind of incident is it?'

'An explosion of some sort, in the region of St Katherine's Dock,' Adam told her. 'You'll be with me. We'll be going to the incident area along with the mobile unit, and we need to put on emergency outfits to denote who we are.' He waved a hand in the direction of the doctors' lounge. 'You'll find them in the locker next to the table.'

He turned towards the reception desk. 'Sarah, you'll be helping out with triage and, Colin, you'll be on standby to receive the injured patients.'

Sarah went to make her own preparations, and Colin hurried away to check on equipment. Hannah was already feeling panicky inside. She had never had to deal with a major incident before, and she hoped that she was up to the task. There were butterflies in her stomach as she followed Adam to the ambulance bay a few minutes later.

'We'll report to the medical incident officer at the scene,' Adam said, as the ambulance took them across the city. 'He'll direct us to where we're needed.' He glanced at her, his dark brows drawing together. 'Are you all right?'

'Yes, I'm fine.' She had to disguise the tremor in her voice. She wasn't all right. She was dreading what they might find, and she was afraid that she wouldn't be able to handle this situation, away from the hospital.

He frowned, but said nothing more. When they arrived at the scene just a short time later, the air was filled with a cacophony of sound, and there were ambulances and police vehicles all around. Heart thumping, Hannah scanned the area, taking in the waters where innumerable boats, cabin cruisers and larger marine vehicles were moored. Beyond the water there was a parade of boutiques, souvenir shops and restaurants. There were tables and chairs set out on the pavement in front of cafés and snack bars, where people could sit and look out over the water. No one was doing that just now, though.

The medical incident officer sent them over to the rear of the main dock area. 'We've some casualties in front of the far building,' he said. 'One of them has a chest injury, and another has a possible neck injury and broken arm. You should see to them first.'

Hannah was puzzled. Perhaps it was a feeling of disorientation, but she was finding all this very confusing. So far, she hadn't come across any debris from the explosion, but when she went round to the area where the incident officer had directed her, she could see that parts of the parade were screened off, and people were lying on the floor, being tended to by doctors and paramedics.

It was a dreadful scene, and her heart went out to those poor people. Police were interviewing people who she assumed had been passers-by when the incident had happened, and they were moving them to one side to quieter areas. Perhaps they feared another explosion.

'You take the chest patient,' Adam said. 'I'll see to the neck injury.'

Hannah nodded, but she was still uncertain. There was something about all this that didn't seem quite right, but she couldn't make out what it was.

She went over to the injured man and found him clutching his chest, making groaning sounds as though he was in pain. 'I'll just make a quick examination,' she told him, 'and then I'll do my best to make you feel more comfortable.'

Adam was fitting a neck brace on his patient, and Hannah carefully ran her stethoscope over the man's chest. Then she took his blood pressure before sitting back, feeling more at a loss than ever.

'Something wrong?' Adam asked, coming over to her.

'Well, not exactly,' she said, moving away from her patient so that she could talk to Adam confidentially. 'To be honest, I can't find anything wrong with him. His chest sounds are fine, and his blood pressure is perfectly normal.'

Adam gave her a quizzical look. 'Yes…and so, what's the problem?'

She tilted her head back to get a better look at him. 'That's what I'm saying. There is no problem.'

'Isn't that what you expected?' His mouth made a wry shape. 'This is a practice session after all.'

'A practice?' She stared at him, her mouth dropping open. 'Do you mean to say that I've been worrying myself silly over nothing…that this whole episode has been set up like something out of a play?'

'That's right.' His grey eyes were watchful. 'Didn't you know? Are you saying that John Tremayne didn't tell you?'

'He didn't tell me.' She felt suddenly deflated and annoyed all at the same time. 'I've been apprehensive since we set out to come here, and now you're telling me that it was all unnecessary. I wish he'd said something. I wish you'd said something. Am I the only one who didn't know?'

'Probably. It must have been an oversight on his part, because of you being new to the hospital. All this was arranged some time ago.' He laid a hand on her shoulder. 'Put it down to experience. At least you'll know what to expect if the real thing ever happens.'

She didn't answer. His hand was warm on her shoulder, and though the gesture was probably meant to be casual and reassuring, she was far too aware of his nearness for her to be able to think straight. The touch of his fingers was sending sparks straight through to her nervous system, and her whole body was fired up in response.

It lasted for just a brief moment in time, though. A second or two later, he released her and said, 'Just treat the patients as though they actually were injured, and send them on their way to hospital for treatment. That's how these things work.'

It had meant nothing to him. For him, the closeness was casual, a fleeting thing, and he was already heading back to his patient.

Hannah took a deep breath and tried to shake off the sensations he had unwittingly stirred up in her. She didn't want to be so conscious of him, so tuned in to his every movement. It had been the same back home when she had been a child. He had made her head spin. She had been constantly aware of him, on edge, her senses thrown into chaos whenever he had been around. As a teenager she had been too unsettled to know what it was that she'd wanted, and, anyway, he was way out of her reach.

Even then, he had represented another world, where his had been a voice of confident authority, his manner towards her tempered with teasing curiosity…until he had allowed himself to become part of the witch hunt that had caused Ryan such distress.

She went back to work, attending to other pseudo-patients. Some half an hour later, though, she had to go and seek him out. 'I need some help here,' she said urgently. 'I'm worried about this patient and I want to get him to hospital right now, but the officer in charge is making me wait until the other casualties have been taken.'

'That's how it works,' Adam said. 'The officer decides who has priority.'

'But this is real,' she insisted. 'I've been trying to explain and no one's taking any notice. I've just examined this man, and his heart rate is way too high, and he's breathless and cyanosed. You should come and take a look at him. His skin is grey and there's a sheen of sweat on his face.'

'It's make-up,' Adam said, 'and he's probably hyperventilating. They try to make these things as realistic as possible.'

'I know that, but you're not listening to me.' She was beginning to feel desperate now. 'Come and see for yourself. I've listened to his chest and there are bubbling sounds in his lungs. I couldn't properly make out what he was saying, but as far as I understand it I think he had a prosthetic heart valve fitted some time ago. I think something has gone wrong with it, and now he has a cardiogenic pulmonary oedema, and he needs to go to hospital right now.'

This time the urgency in her voice must have got through to him, because Adam came with her and knelt down next to the patient. Hannah had propped the man up in order to ease his breathing, and she was giving him oxygen through a mask, but he was in bad shape.

'I've given him frusemide to try to remove some of the fluid from his lungs,' she said, 'and he's had two puffs of glyceryl trinitrate.'

Adam made a swift examination and said quietly, 'Have you given him morphine for the pain?'

She nodded. 'And an anti-emetic.' Her mouth made a straight line. 'We really need to get him into the intensive care unit.'

'I agree with you.' Adam stood up and signalled to a couple of paramedics who came over to join them.

'This man needs to go to hospital immediately,' he said. 'This is a real emergency. This is not part of the practice. He's suffering from heart failure that has come on suddenly—possibly from the failure of a prosthetic valve. I want you to call the hospital and notify the cardiac surgeon. The team will probably need to arrange an emergency echocardiograph and get him to Theatre as soon as possible.'

When Adam spoke, everyone took notice, and at last things started moving. He cut a swathe through the assembled crowd, and the man was transferred to the ambulance within a matter of minutes. Hannah went with him to oversee his treatment on the journey, and Adam sat alongside her.

She was glad of his presence. For all that she was guarded around him, she needed his expertise right now. She had done everything she could to save her patient, but she was still a relatively inexperienced junior doctor, and she wanted Adam by her side to instil her with confidence and reassure her that she was doing the right thing. They were battling against the clock and she was desperately afraid that the man wouldn't make it.

By the time they reached the hospital, they had him hooked up to an ECG monitor and had taken blood for testing. The patient was fighting for his life, and Hannah was worried that they might be too late.

The cardiac surgeon and his team met them at the ambulance bay, and whisked her patient away. Hannah stared after him, her heart racing and a heavy feeling in the pit of her stomach.

'Let him go now,' Adam said, softly. 'You've done all that you can for him.'

'It might not have been enough,' she whispered, 'but I didn't know what else to do. I felt as though I was badly equipped… I didn't have all the facilities of the hospital to hand and I was floundering… It was as though I was helpless.'

'You did everything that was possible. No one expects something like that to happen. On a practice like that, most people are healthy volunteers. You don't imagine that anyone could be seriously ill.'

'He said he thought he had some sort of flu. He'd come on the exercise because he didn't want to let anyone down.' She sent him a swift, sideways glance. 'It didn't faze you, though, did it, having to cope with something out of the ordinary?'

In fact, he had been in his element, cutting through procedural barriers without a second thought, and the patient had been transferred without a hitch.

'I'm used to it. I've had more experience of this sort of thing than you have.' He studied her closely. 'Even so, you seem to be generally on edge, not just on the practice, but here, working in A and E. It's as though you're out of place here. I've sensed it from the beginning, but I suspect there's more to it than simple apprehension about the job. Is it the city that makes you nervous? You don't appear to have settled properly since you arrived.'

She wasn't going to pretend that things were otherwise. 'It's probably a bit of both.' It was difficult to admit it, but the truth was it worried her that she was out of her depth. She needed to be here, but that helpless feeling coloured everything that she did in A and E and hampered her way of life, and she didn't know whether she would ever manage to overcome it. Here in the city, she had that same feeling of being overwhelmed that she had suffered as a child.

She lifted her gaze to him. 'You wouldn't have any understanding of that, would you? You fit into city life as though you were made for it, and your whole family is confident that they've made their mark. Your father's achievements go without saying…your brother has his restaurant, and your sister is a high flier in advertising. They all know who they are and what they are about, but it isn't the same for me. I need to find out who I really am and where I belong.'

He studied her, his gaze thoughtful. 'So you're here to find your natural mother, is that it?'

Her breath caught in her throat. Of course he was bound to guess what she planned to do. She nodded. 'I heard that she'd been in London at some point. I put in a call to a missing persons helpline, and I've come here to see if I can find any information about her locally.'

'I knew there had to be a reason why you were here in the city.' He shook his head. 'I think you're making a mistake. From what I heard, she abandoned you, and never came back to make things up with you. I doubt it will help to have her fecklessness confirmed all over again. Perhaps you should deal with things the way they are and move on.'

His blunt manner was hurtful, but she didn't want him to see the effect his words had on her. Hannah looked at him steadily. 'I didn't really expect you to say anything different. Why would you understand? It's perfectly obvious that we're from totally different worlds. We don't see things the same way. I doubt that we ever will.'

She left him and went to check up on Dean's progress on the medical ward. If Adam was anxious for her to get back to the practice area, that was too bad. She was due for a break, and she needed to put some distance between herself and her one-time neighbour from back home. It helped to think of Adam that way. It smoothed out the ragged edges of her feelings towards him.

CHAPTER THREE

'I'M NOT going to school.' Ellie glowered at her mother. 'I want to stay at home and play with my dollies.' Her mouth set in a mutinous line.

'You have to go to nursery school,' Abby told her. 'I have to go to work today, and the teachers will be waiting for you.'

Hannah heard the exchange as she came out of her flat. As she started downstairs, she saw that her neighbours were standing in the hallway by the front door, and Abby was looking harassed.

'Don't like my teachers,' Ellie stormed. 'They're horrible.'

'Oh, dear.' Hannah glanced at the child and then at Abby. 'It doesn't sound as though she's very happy, today, does it?'

Abby made a face. 'She isn't. Her usual teacher was off school yesterday, and Ellie hasn't taken kindly to her replacement. Apparently she scolded her for snatching a toy from another child, and now Ellie's digging her heels in. She says the boy took it from her first and there was a scuffle, but the truth is, she doesn't take to change very well. It unsettles her.'

'I can imagine it would.' Hannah smiled at Ellie. 'I thought you liked going to school? You have lots of fun making things, and you love to play with the toys, don't you?'

The child didn't answer, but simply stared her out, and Abby sighed and turned to her daughter. 'It's a bright, sunny day today, and they'll probably let you go outside with the bikes and cars,' she murmured. 'You like doing that, don't you?'

Ellie thought about it for a moment, but she wasn't about to give in that easily. She gave a negligent shrug. 'I want to play with the water trough.' She scowled, clearly looking for a negative response.

'I expect you'll be able to do that,' Abby said, unperturbed. 'I'll have a word with your teacher.' She looked down at Ellie, who was nonplussed all at once and appeared to have run out of arguments for the time being. 'Now, we really must go.'

Hannah waved goodbye as they finally set off along the street. She hurried to the underground station, aware that time was running on, and that Adam would not be too pleased if she didn't arrive on time for the start of her shift.

She grimaced. It wasn't easy, working alongside him. As it turned out, he was quite often left in charge while Mr Tremayne was away from the department, and he watched over everything that she did as though he expected her to fall flat on her face at any moment. He was probably right in that. She still hadn't found her feet yet in emergency work, but it made her uneasy to acknowledge that she was out of her depth.

The tube was crowded, and she had to stand for part of the journey. It was an uncomfortable way to travel, standing shoulder to shoulder with other commuters. People jostled her and she had to brace herself as the train picked up speed and the noise level increased as it clattered along the lines and hurtled through the tunnel.

She wondered how Adam travelled to work. Sarah had said that she thought he walked in each morning, and that seemed a reasonable conclusion. Apparently he lived close by and the exercise probably helped to keep him fit.

'Stay away.' The abrupt comment broke into her thoughts, drawing her attention. It was a disjointed, weird sort of sound, and she saw that it came from a man who was a short distance away, seated diagonally opposite her in the carriage. He was talking to himself. His shoulders were hunched and there was an angry expression on his face.

A woman stood up and urged her child towards the doors, getting ready for her stop. As she passed by the young man, he started to shout, hurling abuse at her, and she shrank back, looking apprehensive as she pushed the child behind her, trying to shield him from the onslaught.

'What do you think you're doing?' the man spat out. 'Don't you come near me.'

Hannah moved instinctively, easing herself along the carriage until she had placed herself between the seated passenger and the child and his mother. At all costs, she wanted to protect that child. Tense with foreboding, she positioned her back against a vertical support rail and watched him, trying to categorise his odd behaviour. He was looking around him in agitation, addressing an unseen individual.

'I'll do it…I will,' he muttered, his face clenched with determination. 'I have a knife, you know. I'll use it. I will.'

An older man stood up, and moved to stand beside Hannah. He looked uneasy, guarded, as though he, too, sensed that something untoward might happen, and Hannah said in an undertone, 'Perhaps we should try to find out if there's a security guard travelling with us.'

The man nodded, but didn't move. Perhaps he was worried about leaving her side. He looked as though he was in his mid-sixties, a frail-looking man, whose breathing was wheezy, and Hannah wondered whether between them they would be able to quell any disturbance from the younger man. She didn't see any other choice…no one else in the carriage looked as though they were ready to join in. Instead, the passengers were sending him watchful, suspicious looks.

The unkempt passenger was still seated, but now he drew out a pocketknife, the blade extended, and started to wave it around in the air, the action exuding menace. Hannah sucked in her breath. The mother and child edged closer to the exit doors and Hannah prayed that the train would soon slow down and come into a station. She was keyed up, her heart hammering with frantic, adrenaline-pumped nervous energy, but she wasn't at all sure what to do. Adam would have known how to handle this, she was certain, but he wasn't here, and this was one situation that she had to work out for herself.

'I warned you,' the man growled, leaping to his feet. He lunged towards Hannah, making a downward, slashing movement in the direction of her shoulder, the blade of the knife flashing silver in the artificial light. Instinctively, she swung away from it, steadying herself against the rail with her foot and a hand. With her free arm she tried to ward off the threat, and at the same time the older man made a grab for her attacker's sweater.

Blood rushed to her head and pounded in her ears, making her sway with the motion of the train. She curved her fingers around the support rail and clung on. A moment or two later, when she recovered her senses, she saw the passenger who was in the seat next to the man shoot out of the way in case he was next in line, and someone else had grabbed the knifeman's arm.

There was a scuffle, and between them her fellow travellers managed to subdue the would-be assailant and dislodge his grip on the knife. Hannah breathed a sigh of relief.

'Are you hurt?' the older man asked, struggling for breath, and Hannah shook her head.

'I don't think so.' She looked down at her jacket and saw that the material was sliced through to the thin shoulder pad. 'I think I must have had a lucky escape,' she said, a tremor in her voice.

By now, someone had managed to find the security guard, and as the train braked, pulling into a station, Hannah was thankful to see that the situation was being brought under control. The deranged young man was struggling, but he was held in a firm grip by the passengers.

'I think he ought to see a doctor,' she pointed out as the man was taken away. Even though he had been violent, she was afraid that he might be treated like a common criminal. 'He sounds as though he's delusional, and it could possibly be that he's suffering from some kind of psychosis like schizophrenia. He might need medication to calm him down.'

The security man nodded. 'You're probably right. We'll sort it out. Perhaps you ought to hang around for a while and give a statement to the police.' He indicated his radio transmitter. 'I've arranged for them to meet up with us.'

The woman and child had gone by the time Hannah left the carriage and walked out onto the platform. Perhaps they'd had a lucky escape. She couldn't help thinking that she had only just scraped through unscathed herself. There was no sign of the older man who had stepped in to help her.

She was a few minutes late by the time she finally hurried into the hospital and made her way to the changing room. Still strung out from what had happened just a short time ago, she made an effort to prepare herself for the day ahead. Hanging up her damaged jacket, she prepared to go and check her list of patients.

Adam frowned as she walked towards the reception desk. 'You're late,' he said.

She nodded, 'Yes, I know. I'm sorry.'

He studied her strained features and said with an edge to his voice, 'What was the problem…a heavy night? Too much partying?'

'Nothing like that. There was a problem on the tube.' She thought of the young mother, trying to protect her child, and a sudden surge of recollection swept over her…something her father had once said, about her mother not being capable of looking after a child. She remembered travelling to London with her mother. They had gone to visit her grandmother, but when they'd arrived at the house they had discovered that she had been ill and her mother had been sad.

'Are you still with us?' Adam roused her from her reverie. He appeared sceptical, but said, 'Since you're here at last, could you see to the patient in treatment room three? He has a facial injury that needs stitching.'

She went to see her patient, and started to carefully examine the gash that disfigured his cheek. Even now, though, her hands were shaking in the aftermath of the incident on the underground. It was beginning to dawn on her that she had come within inches of being knifed, and the realisation brought her out in a cold sweat. She knew that she was in no state to suture this wound. It would need a far steadier hand than hers.

'Excuse me,' she said to her patient, 'while I go and have a word with a colleague. You'll need some stitches in there. It's a nasty wound, but with any luck you should heal fine and be left with only a faint scar.'

She went in search of Colin. He looked surprised when she asked him to take over for her, but he didn't query it, apart from asking, 'I suppose it's coming in late that's thrown you? Perhaps you should go and get a coffee before you make a start. You might feel better after that.'

Her mouth made a weak smile. 'Thanks,' she said. 'I'll be all right in a while.'

Coffee sounded like a good idea, and it might help to soothe her nerves, or at least the caffeine might give her a boost. Perhaps she could slip away without Adam paying her any attention.

It was easier said than done, though. When she went into the doctors' lounge, she discovered that Adam was there before her. He was half-turned from her, talking to someone whose face was hidden from her momentarily, but just as she would have backed out of the room, the man moved into her line of sight.

'Your sister was hoping you'd be able to go along to her celebration dinner,' Monroe Driscoll was saying. 'Her luck's changing. She's brought off a real coup with this advertising account, and she wanted us all to share in her good fortune.'

'I don't think luck had much to do with it,' Adam murmured. 'She worked hard on that presentation and she deserved to secure it.'

He turned and flicked a frowning glance over Hannah. 'You can't have finished with your patient already, can you?'

'Colin is attending to him. He's much better at suturing facial wounds than I am.'

His mouth made a straight line. 'I doubt that. Perhaps you'd better go and get yourself a hot drink. It might make you feel better.' He looked at her closely, his eyes narrowing momentarily, but then he shifted his gaze back to his father and said, 'You remember Hannah, don't you?' To Hannah, he added, 'My father's in London for a business meeting.'

Monroe stared at her. 'Good heavens…it *is* Hannah, isn't it? I suppose I should have recognised you with that mass of golden curls.' His mouth indented briefly as he looked her over. 'I thought you would go to work in the village, perhaps take up a post in the local college or some such. This is the last place I imagined I would find you.'

'I wanted to complete my training here,' she said. She went over to the coffee machine and poured herself a drink. She didn't know which was worse, having a narrow escape from being attacked or meeting up with Monroe Driscoll. Her foster-brother would be appalled. Clasping her fingers around the mug at least helped to settle her nerves a little. 'The emergency department here has a good reputation.'

'Yes, I heard that. It was one of the reasons that made Adam decide to come here, I believe. Of course, he's been working to obtain extra specialist qualifications, and once he has a consultant's post, the opportunities will be second to none.'

Hannah glanced towards Adam. 'I guessed that was what you were aiming for,' she murmured. 'Will you apply for a post here?'

Adam nodded. 'I've already made the application. That's partly why I'm standing in for Mr Tremayne a lot of the time. He's thinking of moving to the South Coast.'

'Is he? I didn't know that.' The news wasn't what she wanted to hear. Surely the consultant wasn't thinking of moving on in the next few weeks? That would mean that Adam would be in charge all the time until they found a replacement. She took a sip of her coffee and felt the hot liquid warm her through and through, reviving her spirits a little.

'What made you decide to join the medical profession?' Monroe asked. 'I have difficulty imagining you coping with the everyday drama of it, let alone getting involved with emergency work.'

Did he, too, think she was hopeless? What was it with these Driscoll men? 'I've wanted to be a doctor ever since Ryan was ill with meningitis,' she said. She took another swallow from her mug and hoped that it would calm her down. 'It was a frightening time, and at one stage we even thought he might die, but the doctors managed to pull him through.'

'Ah, yes…Ryan. I remember how worried your mother was at that time.' He made a grimace. 'In fact, she always seemed to have more than her share of worries over him, what with his misdemeanours and his scrapes with the wrong side of the law.'

Hannah stiffened. 'He had a troubled background and he was feeling his way for a time. What he needed was help, not censure.'

'Perhaps he's managed to turn things around,' Adam intervened. 'I heard that he was looking for work hereabouts.'

Hannah opened her mouth to reply, but Sarah pushed open the door and said, 'Hannah, there's a patient out here with breathing difficulties. I think he needs to be seen right away.'

'I'm on my way.' Hannah rinsed out her mug, and turned to face Adam's father once more. 'I hope your meeting goes well.'

'Thank you.' Monroe inclined his head in acknowledgement. 'It was good to see you again.'

Hannah doubted that. For her, it had been a shock, coming across him this way, but perhaps he would soon be gone. It wouldn't be quite so easy to rid herself of the memory of the way he had treated Ryan.

She hurried to see her patient. To her surprise, it was the older man from the tube, the man who had grabbed her attacker. The nurse was giving him oxygen through a mask but he was still struggling to get his breath.

'Mr Harry Whittaker,' she said, glancing briefly at his chart, and then back at the patient. 'I'm Dr Bennett. I'm so sorry to see that you're not well. I've been wanting to thank you for helping me this morning.' She glanced at his notes once more. 'It says here that you suffer from asthma…is that right?'

He nodded. 'I didn't realise…that you…worked here,' he said, but his breathing was so laboured that it was clear it was difficult for him to speak.

Hannah smiled at him. 'I'm going to take care of you. Don't worry…and don't try to talk. We'll try to make you more comfortable.'

Sarah drew her to one side and said quietly, 'His peak expiratory flow is half what he says his usual reading is. When I first took his pulse it was 110, but then it started falling, until it was below normal. He's becoming exhausted very fast.'

Hannah nodded. 'Let's get an arterial blood-gas

measurement, and we'll put him on nebulised salbu-
tamol.' She turned back to her patient. 'I'm going to
give you a steroid to help you through this, Harry,' she
told him.

Some time later it was clear that his condition wasn't
improving. 'We'll add another bronchodilator…iprat-
ropium…to the nebuliser,' Hannah told Sarah, 'and I'll
make arrangements to admit him.'

Adam came to find out what was happening. 'Is
something wrong here?' he asked.

Hannah quickly explained the situation to him. 'He
hasn't been responding to the treatment, and I'm worried
about his overall condition, given his age. I would have
expected some change for the better by now.'

'Maybe…but it's possible that he's been under par
for some time before this. He isn't young any more.
Perhaps you shouldn't expect immediate results.'

'I realise that, but I saw him earlier this morning
when I was on my way to work. He didn't look too well
then, but I can see that he's in a much worse state now.'

'Give the ipratropium a few more minutes. After
that, you could try an intravenous infusion of aminophylline,' Adam said. 'That should help.'

She nodded. 'I'll do that.' She glanced at him. 'I
take it that your father's gone, then?'

'That's right.' His expression was sombre. 'From
the cool reception you gave him, I guess you two still
have issues to resolve?'

Her mouth tightened. 'I doubt you would understand. You've always sided with your father. Neither of
you had much time for my foster-brother.'

'I'd say Ryan brought that on himself, wouldn't you?'

She didn't answer. Instead, she went to check on her patient. His blood pressure and heart rate were giving her cause for concern, and she was beginning to wonder whether she would need to intubate him.

Adam came to supervise the infusion of aminophylline. 'Make it a slow infusion over twenty minutes,' he said. To Harry, he added, 'This should relax the air passages and help you to breathe more easily.'

Harry nodded.

Adam looked at his chart. 'Are you making arrangements to admit him to a ward?' he asked Hannah.

'Yes, that's all in hand.'

'Good. I'll come back in a little while to see how he's doing.'

Hannah checked the infusion, and then went to deal with another patient. She was calmer now, and more in control of herself, and bit by bit the morning's incident was receding from her thoughts. The mother and child were safe, and she was thankful for that.

Adam came to monitor Harry's condition a few minutes later, as he had promised. Harry was more alert now, and his heart rate had improved.

'How are you feeling now, Harry?' Adam asked. 'Is the breathing any better?'

Harry nodded. 'It's a lot easier. Thanks.'

'We're going to keep you in hospital overnight, at least, but we need to sort out why this happened,' Adam murmured. 'Did anything in particular bring this on, do you know?' He laid a hand on the man's shoulder. 'There's no rush for you to answer. Take your time.'

Harry lifted the oxygen mask a fraction. 'There was a man…on the tube. He had a knife.'

Adam frowned. 'You weren't hurt, were you?' He looked concerned all at once. 'I wasn't aware that you had any injuries.'

Harry shook his head. 'Not me. He went for her.' Harry pointed a finger at Hannah and then pulled on the oxygen. 'She…knocked his arm away. Couldn't let him try again…grabbed him.'

Adam's eyes widened. He stared at Hannah and then turned back to Harry. 'I had no idea about any of this… Was anyone hurt?'

Once more, Harry shook his head. 'Lucky escape.'

Adam nodded. 'I think I can see that now.' He patted his shoulder. 'I'm going to leave you in the care of our nurse, and I want you to try to get some rest. I think you've had quite enough excitement for one day, but I do want to thank you for saving our Dr Bennett. I can see now why she's been giving you special attention. You concentrate on yourself now, and take care.'

Hannah watched him with Harry. He was gentle, watchful and more than considerate of his patient's well-being. This was the Adam she had always known, and her heart swelled with respect and admiration for him.

It was a short-lived feeling, though. When Adam turned and drew her away from the bedside, his manner was grim.

'I can see now why you were late coming in to work this morning,' he said. 'Did it not occur to you to tell me what had happened?'

She shook her head. 'It was all a bit overwhelming, to be honest, and I needed to think things through.' She hesitated. 'The man was a schizophrenic, I think. His behaviour was irrational and unpredictable, and we all had to act quickly.'

Adam's brows lifted. 'What was all that about a knife?'

'It was all over in a matter of minutes, really. He made a lunge at me, but between them the other passengers stopped him. Harry was brilliant.'

'It's no wonder you were in such a state first thing.' His expression was harsh. 'You should have told me. I'm your supervisor and I should know what's going on, and whether you're capable of doing your job. I don't expect to find these things out at second hand.'

'I'm sorry.' Hannah pressed her lips together. 'I felt a bit foolish, to be honest. I wasn't expecting anything like that to happen and it made me a bit jittery for a while.' She thought about the mother and child and the memories they had evoked of her own childhood. Who had been there to protect her through her early years? Had her father been right when he'd said her mother hadn't been capable? 'I think I'd much rather travel to work on a cranky old bus, trundling along country lanes,' she murmured.

'Yes, I can imagine you would be happier doing that,' he said. 'We all know that you would be far more at home in the countryside than you are here.'

It hurt, hearing him say that, even though he was probably right. Her whole world was unsettling and confusing. Even her plans to find her real mother had gone astray. She hadn't been able to find any trace of her so far, and it was beginning to look as though she would have to pursue other alternatives.

Where she might have hoped to look to Adam for support, it simply wasn't going to happen. She had no choice but to stand alone and take care of herself.

CHAPTER FOUR

'THERE's more toast if you want it, Ryan,' Hannah said, pouring coffee for both of them. She glanced at her foster-brother. 'You've not eaten very much. Are you taking proper care of yourself? You're looking thinner than you were last time I saw you.'

'Yes, *Mum*. I'm looking after myself.' Ryan gave her a cheeky grin. 'You've stuffed me with eggs and bacon, and I'm actually full up. You don't have to worry about me.'

'If you say so.' She smiled at him. 'It's lovely that you were able to come and visit me, and I just wish that I was free to spend more time with you.'

He shrugged. 'I know that you have to work. It's all right. It's what I expected, but I thought, since I don't have to be in college for a few days, I could come down to the city and spend some time with you. I can study just as easily here as I can out in Enfield, and it's a more pleasant prospect than staying in my room at the college.'

'Well, even here, you shouldn't stay in all day. You'll

feel better if you can manage to go out and get some fresh air for a while.'

She sent another quick, searching look in his direction. His wavy black hair was pushed back, as though he had been running his fingers through it, and his brown eyes were troubled. For all that he was putting up a brave front, he wasn't his usual self, that was for sure, but so far he hadn't given her even a hint of what was wrong. She knew him well enough to be certain that something untoward was going on. 'It might cheer you up if you can get out and about a bit and see some of the sights.'

He nodded. 'I thought I might do that. I came across your neighbour, Abby, last night, while I was waiting for you to come home, and we stopped to talk for a few minutes. I told her that I was studying countryside management and forestry, and she suggested that I go and visit the Old Park Wood behind Harefield Hospital.'

Hannah was thoughtful for a moment. 'I think she said that she used to live near there. It's probably a good idea. It's a nice warm day, and it shouldn't take you too long to get there.'

'It's worth a visit, isn't it? She said that this time of year the woods look lovely with bluebells and wood anemones, and even some more unusual plants. There's a pond and a stream, and there are different varieties of trees—oak, birch, hornbeam and ash, from what she remembered—so there are probably different soil types, and it might actually help with my studies if I go along and take a look.'

'I think you're probably right.'

He made a small grimace. 'It seems as though I've been cooped up for a long time, and I could do with a break. The exams aren't for a while yet, so I still have a bit of breathing space.'

He was quiet for a moment, mulling things over, and then he added, 'I could come with you as far as the hospital and then go on from there, if that's all right with you? I don't think it will be too far out of my way, and I'll be able to call in on a student friend while I'm in the city.'

'It sounds good to me. I'm glad that you're making plans for the day. Will your friend go with you to look at the woods, do you think?'

'I doubt it. He's having a few problems and he's ditched his course halfway through. As far as I know, he's managed to find some temporary work in London, so I thought I'd check up on how he's doing.'

She was glad to know that he was keeping in touch with his friends. For all his troubled background, Ryan was good at heart. She believed in him.

He said lightly, 'You haven't told me much about your job at the hospital. Is it going well? Are you getting on all right with the people you're working with?'

'I haven't had time to get to know them all yet, but on the whole they seem to be really friendly.' Hannah was quiet for a moment or two, wondering how she was going to break it to him that she was working with Adam. 'The job itself is quite a challenge. I'm still feeling my way, for the most part.'

Ryan studied her. 'There's something you're not telling me. Are you having a problem of some sort?'

She shook her head. 'No, it's nothing like that.' She hesitated, and then added, 'Actually, I'm working with Adam Driscoll. He's the specialist registrar in A and E, so for quite a lot of the time he's my supervisor. He's in charge when the consultant isn't available.'

Ryan stared at her. Then he seemed to gather himself together and said, grimacing, 'That must have come as a bit of a shock. I know I certainly wouldn't want to be working with him...I'd always be watching my back in case something went wrong and I was caught up in the middle of it. I've had bitter experience of his family's peculiar brand of justice.'

He frowned. 'I can't say that I'm surprised he's in charge, though. He's always been ambitious, and I would imagine he's aiming for a post as consultant himself. He wouldn't be one to let the grass grow under his feet.'

Hannah nodded. 'I heard talk that he's taking the exams and publishing work that will qualify him for a consultant position. Rumour has it that he'll be moving on after that.' That didn't surprise her either. Ever since she had known Adam he had been steadfastly edging towards success.

She began to clear away the breakfast crockery, while Ryan busied himself folding up the duvet he had used last night, and then he converted the simple sofa bed back into a couch. A few minutes later they were ready to leave.

He went with her as far as the entrance to the A and E department, and she helped him to work out how he was going to get to the woods later on. 'It looks as though you'll need to take the Metropolitan Line,' she murmured, glancing at her map of the underground.

He nodded, but she saw that he was looking a little subdued, and she said hesitantly, 'Are you bothered about going on your own? Maybe you and I could go together another day, or perhaps Abby and her little girl might like a trip out there after she finishes work?'

'No, she can't manage it. I already asked... I don't really know her, but she was looking a bit down, and I sort of felt it was the right thing to do, especially since she was the one who told me about it. As it turns out, she's working all day today. It doesn't worry me, being on my own. I'm fine.'

She looked at him. 'I don't think you're fine at all. I know that something's bothering you. Do you want to talk about it? Are you worried about the exams?'

'No, it isn't anything to do with my course.' He looked uncomfortable, obviously diffident about saying any more.

'Is it money?' she asked. 'I can let you have some to tide you over...'

'I don't want you to do that. Anyway, I've enough to last me for a while. I might apply for an extension to my student loan.'

She frowned. 'Are you sure?'

His mouth made an odd shape. 'I'm all right for the time being, anyway.' He was quiet for a moment, but then seemed to come to a decision and said reluctantly, 'The truth is, my landlord's threatening to take me to court...he's complaining about damage to property of some sort, and on top of that there have been threatening letters from the television rental company and one or two other companies that are getting tough with me over non-payment of bills.' He straightened his shoulders. 'I don't really know what it's all about, but I'll sort it out somehow.'

It didn't make any sense to Hannah. She had thought Ryan's troublemaking, rebellious years were behind him, and this wasn't the sort of difficulty he would normally get into. Something was definitely wrong. She reached out and gave him a hug.

'We'll sort it out together,' she said. 'We'll talk about it after I finish work, and I'll do whatever I can to help.'

Ryan nodded, but then he stiffened, his eyes darkening, and she looked around, following the direction of his gaze.

'Hello, Ryan,' Adam said. His grey gaze flicked over the pair of them, taking in their close embrace. 'I didn't realise that you were in London. Are you staying hereabouts?'

'I'm staying with Hannah. It's just a temporary arrangement,' Ryan answered coolly.

Hannah let her arms drop to her sides, and she drew back from him. The two men were regarding each other with marked suspicion, an undercurrent of hostility flowing between them, each one guarded and standing his ground.

'How have things been going for you?' Adam asked. 'Have you found a job that suits you?'

'I'm not working,' Ryan answered. 'But, then, you'd know all about that, wouldn't you? Wasn't that what you expected after your father threw me out on my ear and told me not to go anywhere near his place again? Neither of you had any time for me. You kicked me out and thought that I would roll all the way downhill.'

'I don't think it was quite like that,' Adam murmured. 'It was a long time ago, and you were very young. You were never meant to be working on the estate in a permanent capacity.'

'And that would be because you didn't think I was good enough, wouldn't it? Your family wanted to scrape me off their boots and throw me on the scrap heap.'

Adam didn't answer, but inclined his head in Hannah's direction and said, 'I'm going into A and E. You and I are going out with the air ambulance today, so you should get ready. We leave in half an hour.'

Hannah froze. This was the first she had heard of it, and the news threw her into an immediate state of turmoil. She had already shown that she was no good in situations outside the hospital. She felt as though she was inadequate and inexperienced away from the security of the hospital and all its facilities. He knew that, so why was he doing this to her?

Adam strode away, and Hannah turned to Ryan, her expression bleak. 'I have to go,' she said. 'Don't concern yourself over what happened before. His family didn't understand how things were with us, and perhaps they overreacted. I know that you've done nothing wrong.'

'That's because you're an angel and you see good in everyone.' He gave her an affectionate look. 'You've been my guiding light over the years, Hannah. I've been thankful for your inner strength and your loyalty.'

She hugged him again, briefly, and said softly, 'We'll

talk later. Try not to dwell on what was in the past. That's over and done with and you're making a fresh start.'

He walked away, and Hannah turned and went into A and E. She had problems of her own right now, and Adam's words had sent her adrenaline into overdrive.

She went into the changing room and pulled on the uniform over-trousers and jacket and then went to find him.

He was by the desk, studying the day's staffing schedule, but he glanced up as she came towards him. 'Good, you're ready,' he said. 'We'll head up to the air ambulance landing pad.' He started towards the lift, and ushered her inside.

'You didn't tell me that I would be doing this today,' she said, her mouth a little stiff.

'That's because I had to revise the schedules last night. Colin is off sick, and so I put you in his place. I thought this would be good practice for you. We all do a week or so with the air ambulance. It's good experience.'

'If you say so.' She pulled in a deep breath as the lift doors opened and they came out onto the flat roof of the hospital. The helicopter was there, waiting for them, and the paramedics were busy checking over their equipment. This was not going to be one of her best days, she could feel it in her bones. She hated anything to do with flying, and a helicopter was the worst option, but she wasn't going to tell him that.

'I do. We just have to wait here for a while, until they're ready to leave.' He threw her a sideways look. 'It came as a bit of a surprise to meet up with your foster-brother again after all this time. I suppose he must have felt much the same way and maybe that's why he was a touch abrasive in his manner. I'm guessing he still bears a grudge?'

'You could be right. He's had a difficult life, one way and another. I don't suppose things will smooth out without the odd crease showing up here and there.'

'That's true enough.' He frowned. 'I didn't mean to butt in on your conversation with him, but I couldn't help overhearing that he's landed himself in a spot of bother…with his landlord and others.'

Her gaze narrowed on him. 'You sound as though that doesn't surprise you.'

'I suppose it doesn't. He had a chequered past, and he didn't really have much of a chance from the beginning, did he? His parents were often in trouble with the law, and he was obviously influenced by them to some extent. It's hardly surprising that he turned into a rebellious teenager, and maybe he's still having problems even now.'

'He isn't a teenager any more. He's a grown man, and he's changed.'

'Has he?' He let his glance travel over her, skimming along the mass of her bright curls and coming to rest on the flushed curve of her cheek. 'You're very close, you and he, aren't you? You're very quick to come to his defence, yet there's no blood tie between you to hold you together, is there? He isn't your real brother, yet you've kept in touch over all these years.'

'It doesn't matter that there's no blood tie. We grew up together, from when we were both starting out as teenagers at least. As I recall, Ryan was fourteen when he came to live at my foster-home, and I was just thirteen. We had a lot in common. We both came from broken homes, and we were just two vulnerable children trying to find our way through the maze. We learned to stick together and look out for each other.'

'You're still doing that now, aren't you?' His expression was cynical. 'You don't see any wrong in him.'

'I see the troubled child. He was only seventeen when he went to work for your father, and he still had a lot to learn. I don't think either of you were fair to him. You judged him without giving him a fair hearing.'

Adam's jaw firmed. 'I don't see how you can say that. He might have coped reasonably well when he was working on the main part of the estate, but as soon as he was put in a position of trust, where he had to handle money, things started to go wrong. I don't believe my father had any choice but to let him go.'

'Didn't he?' Her blue eyes challenged him. 'There were other youths working in the farm shop. I didn't see them coming under fire.'

'That's the point, isn't it? You weren't there. You didn't see what happened, or hear the arguments that went on, so how can you put forward a valid excuse for him? Your opinion is biased and you'll defend him to the last.'

'And you don't think that you're biased the other way?'

'What's that supposed to mean?'

'You know what it means. Your family has always thought badly of Ryan. You saw a delinquent boy, and now you see a man who can do no good. You'll always think the worst of him.'

A paramedic came towards them, and Adam's answer was cut off in the alert to a callout. 'There's been a traffic accident in the city,' the paramedic said, 'and it will take too long to bring the casualties in by road. We're getting ready to leave now.'

Hannah ran with Adam towards the helicopter. Inside, she was worried about what would greet them when they set down, and to some extent that helped her to overcome her fears about the flight. She concentrated on breathing deeply and trying to keep a clear head.

'Have you never been in a helicopter before?' Adam asked.

She blinked and shook her head. 'How did you know?'

His mouth made a crooked slant. 'It must be something to do with your pale face and your white knuckles…along with the closed eyes, of course. You look like a novice traveller.'

'That would be true,' she admitted, risking a quick glance in his direction. She was trying not to look down at the panorama of the city laid out beneath her. It was enough that the helicopter was swinging out in a wide arc, heading towards their destination.

When they finally arrived, she unbuckled herself from her seat and stood up, swaying momentarily. It felt as though her head was spinning, and she steadied herself, resting a hand on the back of her seat.

'Take your time,' Adam said. His hand cupped her elbow, supporting her, and he waited with her for a few seconds while she got herself together.

'I'm all right,' she mumbled, not looking at him. She didn't want her weakness and imperfections laid out for him, and she wasn't sure which was the more unsettling, the helicopter ride or the firm clasp of his hand on her arm. Either way, she was thrown out of kilter.

Adam let her go as soon as he saw that she was able to go on, and as they approached the site of the accident she threw a swift glance around, taking in the wreckage that lay before them. There were several mangled cars, and an ambulance was already standing by, its light flashing. The police were on hand, too, putting up road-blocks, and Hannah hurried over to where the paramedics from the ambulance indicated.

Her first patient was struggling to breathe because of his injuries, and she worked with the paramedic to clear his airway.

Suction didn't help a great deal, and she said, 'There's so much swelling that I can't intubate. I'll do a needle cricothyroidotomy and see if I can buy time for him that way.'

She passed a needle and cannula at a forty-five degree angle through the lower half of the cricothyroid membrane into the trachea. 'I'm in,' she murmured after a while, and then she began to withdraw the needle while advancing the cannula down into position. 'OK, now I need to connect the cannula to the oxygen supply.'

As soon as that was done and she had managed to stabilise her patient, she organised his transfer to the air ambulance.

Adam was working with another injured man, and Hannah turned her attention to a young woman, who had been moved out of her vehicle to a grassy verge by the roadside. The paramedic said that the woman's name was Jessica, and added, 'She has a chest injury, but she didn't seem to be as badly injured as the others, and we had to move her because of the risk of fire. She has been conscious the whole time. We're giving her oxygen because she was having some trouble with her breathing.'

'OK, thanks.'

Hannah went over to the woman and knelt down beside her. 'How are you feeling, Jessica?' she asked, swiftly checking her over. There was a deep wound across the woman's upper chest, and she didn't look as though she was doing too well. Her consciousness level seemed to be slipping, so that Hannah was worried that there might be more wrong with her than was at first obvious.

'My little girl's in the car,' the woman said, ignoring Hannah's question, her voice threaded with anxiety, her breathing laboured. 'I don't think they heard me before with all the noise of the cutting equipment.' She struggled for breath. 'I need to know that she's all right.'

Hannah looked around, concerned all at once. 'Which car?' she asked.

'The…red one…' The woman's voice faded away, and she slumped a little. Hannah glanced up at the paramedic.

'We didn't see anyone in there,' he said, his features suddenly strained. 'I searched the back of the car myself. I'll go and take another look.'

Hannah nodded. She already feared the worst, and it was a heavy feeling, like sickness in her stomach, churning and cloying in her throat. There was no sound coming from the car, as far as she could tell, and the metalwork was mangled and crushed inwards. It was hard to believe that anyone could have survived in the back seat.

'They're going to look for her now,' she said quietly to the young woman. 'Let me take a look at you, to make sure that there's nothing we've missed.'

Jessica's lips moved, but Hannah couldn't make out what she was saying.

Adam came over to her and waited while she finished making a swift examination. He drew her to one side, saying quietly, 'We're waiting to take off. Can you leave this patient to be taken to hospital by the first ambulance crew? She's not as badly injured as the others by all accounts and our patients need to go now. The pilot's getting ready to take off.'

'Just give me another minute, will you?' she answered, keeping her voice low. 'I'm not happy with Jessica's condition. I know that she looked all right to begin with, but now she seems to be deteriorating, and I've no real indication why, just at the moment.'

'What makes you think there's anything untoward happening here? I just spoke to the paramedic. Is it possible that her anxiety about her daughter is making her stressed and giving her the appearance of having a more serious medical condition?'

'No, I don't believe so.' Hannah wasn't ready to give in. 'I just have a bad feeling about this. Her blood pressure is falling, and there's a tachycardia. I'm convinced that she's going into shock, and it's all happening too fast.'

'Then you need to get some fluids into her,' Adam said, turning his attention to the patient.

Hannah nodded. She set about obtaining intravenous access, and started the woman on fluids to counteract hypovolaemic shock. Turning back to Adam, she said, 'I don't want to leave her here. I may be wrong, but I think she's suffered a much worse injury than we at first thought. I'm afraid that if you leave without her, it will take too long for her to get to hospital by road, and she'll suffer as a result.'

She expected an argument from him, because after all she was a very inexperienced doctor, and her opinion probably counted for very little in the grand scheme of things.

Instead, he signalled for the paramedics to bring a trolley over, and started to make arrangements for Jessica to be transferred to the waiting helicopter. 'We'll try and make room for her somehow.'

Just then, coming out of the blue, they heard a shout. The paramedic, who had gone to look for the child, emerged from the other side of the road. 'She's here,' he said. 'The little girl is over here.'

He straightened, and Hannah saw that he was carrying the child. She looked to be about two years old, and she was still firmly strapped into a child's car seat.

'The fixing bolts must have come loose or sheared off,' he said, 'and the jolt of the accident must have thrown her clean out of the car when the door flew open. She looks fine, except for a few scratches.'

Hannah stroked Jessica's arm briefly. 'Did you hear that, Jessica? They've found your little girl. As far as I know, she's all right.' There was no sound from the child, but that could simply mean that she was bewildered, or even that she had been sleeping.

Jessica tried to say something, but it was clear that she was fading fast and the effort was becoming too much for her. Her breathing was becoming more difficult by the minute, and a film of sweat had broken out on her brow. Hannah intubated her to protect her airway, and then stepped back to allow the paramedics to transfer the woman to the helicopter.

Hannah went with them, anxious to see her patient to safety. 'I was thinking there might be a liver or spleen injury,' she told Adam, 'but I'm wondering if there could have been some damage from a broken rib. The clavicle looks to be out of line, and I'm afraid that she's bleeding internally, perhaps from a nipped blood vessel.'

Adam nodded. 'It's possible that a broken rib or the clavicle has been pushed downwards and caused a tear in the aorta.' His expression was grim. 'Few people survive an injury to the heart's main artery.'

A sudden wailing started up behind them, and Hannah glanced around. The child had woken up with a vengeance, and was distraught at seeing her mother being taken away.

'Don't you take my mummy,' she screamed. 'Mummy, Mummy…don't you take my mummy away.'

Hannah tried not to let the heart-rending sound

distract her. The paramedic was trying to soothe the child, but the little girl would not be pacified, and Hannah knew more than ever that she had to keep this woman alive at all costs. She could not let this child be motherless.

Inside the helicopter, she fretted all the way to the hospital. She took a sample of blood from Jessica for cross-matching and tests and she asked the pilot to call ahead to the hospital and arrange for the trauma team to be advised of a possible aortic rupture.

'Is there any chance for her at all?' she asked Adam in a subdued voice. It was clear now that Jessica was fighting for her life.

'It depends on how large the tear is, or whether it has been contained by the adventitia or the mediastinal structures. If she survives long enough to undergo surgery, they might be able to put things right.' He looked at her. 'You've done everything that you can.'

'Have I?' She pressed her lips together. 'It doesn't feel as though it's anywhere near enough.'

As soon as the air ambulance landed, the trauma team rushed forward, whisking the patients down to A and E.

Hannah waited nervously in the emergency room, feeling at a loss, desperate for any news of the young mother. She was glad that there had been no calls for the air ambulance to set off once more. She had to know what was happening here.

'They're still doing tests,' Adam told her when he came back from checking on his patient, 'but they've done a chest X-ray and a CT scan. It looks as though it wasn't a complete tear, but it happened at the aortic isthmus, as we suspected.'

'What happens now?' Hannah was apprehensive. 'I know that, even if she comes through the operation, with some surgery repair techniques the patient can suffer dangerous after-effects, especially if the artery has to be clamped for too long. She isn't out of the woods by a long way, is she?'

'No, she isn't, but there's nothing more you can do for her now.'

Hannah moved restlessly, pacing the room, her hands clenching and unclenching. Until she knew that Jessica had survived, she was fit for nothing. Adam was watching her closely, and he must be thinking that she was a wreck and not fit to be part of the A and E team, but there was nothing she could do to change his opinion of her. She was too strung out to settle.

'Let's go and take a break outside for a few minutes,' he suggested. 'Sarah will let us know as soon as there's any news.'

Hannah didn't have it in her to argue. She went outside with him, and they found a quiet place in the hospital grounds, where they sat under the delicate shade of a birch tree and swallowed coffee from polystyrene cups. It tasted awful, and she pushed it to one side, abandoning it to the flat surface of the bench seat.

Adam sat beside her. 'You look as though you're about to burst into tears,' he said softly, moving closer. 'You shouldn't feel badly about this, you know. You were quick to spot that things weren't right, and it's thanks to your actions that she even made it to hospital.'

'But she isn't safe yet, is she?' Despite all her efforts to stop it, a tear escaped and slid slowly down her cheek. She brushed it away with the back of her hand, ashamed of her weakness. 'I just feel for that little child, calling out for her mother. It twisted at my heart and made me want to hold her and comfort her. I couldn't bear it if she was to lose her.'

Adam studied her thoughtfully. 'I imagine this must be a much more difficult situation for you to handle than it would be for anyone else…given the way things were for you back home. It must remind you of how things were when you were small.'

She stared up at him. Her mouth trembled. 'I don't know. I suppose that could be it. I hadn't thought…' How was it that he was able to see so much?

Another tear escaped, and this time Adam reached out and gently stroked it away with his thumb. His touch was feather light and the warm sensation of his hand resting on her cheek made her yearn for something out of her reach, something that she couldn't even define.

'Do you remember your mother leaving you when you were little?' he asked. His voice was low and coaxing, gently encouraging her to talk to him.

She nodded. 'Yes, I think so. I remember some of it as though it happened only yesterday.' She pulled in a shuddery breath. 'Seeing that little girl brought it all back to me, all those horrible emotions—the fear of being left behind, of seeing my mother going away. I remember that I wanted her to stay with me and I didn't know what was happening. I think I must have been a little older than Jessica's child at the time. They told me she was ill. I cried for my mother, and then my father came from somewhere.'

She frowned. 'I think by then I was being looked after by a friend of the family, and when my father came and talked to me, I wasn't sure who he was. Anyway, he said he couldn't have me to stay with him. They told me that it was because he had just married again and it was the wrong time.'

She sniffed and swallowed the tears that caught in the back of her throat. 'Of course, I didn't really understand. I just thought that this was my daddy, that's what they told me, and yet here he was, saying that he didn't want me.' Her voice cracked. 'I was sure that there must be something wrong with me.'

Adam's arm slid around her. 'That must have been terrible for you. It's no wonder that you're upset. These things stay with you for a lifetime, don't they?'

She didn't answer. Instead, she fumbled in her pocket and brought out a clean tissue. Carefully, with shaking fingers, she dabbed at her face. 'I'm sorry,' she said. 'I shouldn't have laid my troubles on you.'

'I'm glad that you did,' he murmured. 'I only wish that I could change things for you and make the past disappear, but I can't do that.' He leaned towards her, his arms holding her close, drawing her to him so that her forehead rested lightly against his cheek. He was gentle and tender towards her, as though he would sweep all her worries away and make her forget that they had ever existed.

She was thankful for his soothing presence, for his

calm and quiet manner. She needed this gentleness, this closeness, this warm feeling of belonging, just as a parched flower needed rain, but it made her long for more, so much more.

It was bound not to last, and steadily the world began to intrude. She became aware of noises in the distance, of the sound of traffic on the main road some way beyond them, and there was the clatter of a trolley, the clank of something being unloaded in the far bay.

She came to her senses slowly and blinked, trying to adjust to the cold world of reality, but Adam was already easing himself away from her.

'Are you feeling a bit better now, a little more ready to face the world?' he asked softly. He was looking at her with a guarded expression.

Hannah nodded and drew away from him. 'I shouldn't have involved you in my problems that way,' she said. 'It won't happen again.' She straightened up. 'I didn't mean to crumple like that. I wasn't thinking straight. I just wasn't thinking at all.'

If she had been, she would surely have kept her distance from him. After all, he was the last person who should get to see her vulnerable side. They were on opposite sides of the fence, and Ryan would readily testify to that.

She could see from the darkening of his eyes that he must be thinking along the same lines. He had been full of compassion for her and he had wanted to console her and reassure her so that she would be strong enough to go on, but things had gone just a little too far for comfort, hadn't they? He must already be regretting his expression of sympathy towards her. The closeness had been one step too far.

She might get the wrong idea, and there was no way that Adam wanted to become entangled with her. What on earth had she been thinking, cosying up to him that way?

'If you're feeling better,' he said, 'we should be getting ready to go back to work.'

She nodded. 'Yes, I'm all right. I'm ready to go now.' She glanced up at him. He looked...what was it that his features showed? Relief? Thankfulness that things were back to normal? It was impossible to say.

She walked with him into the hospital once more, and it was as though nothing had happened between them. He was professional all at once, his mind directed totally towards work. She didn't know what to make of him, but perhaps it was better that way.

CHAPTER FIVE

HANNAH stepped out of the lift and turned to walk along the hospital corridor. She had wasted an hour or more that morning, following up on another false lead in the search for her mother, and even the news that Dean was getting better couldn't lessen the disappointment of that failure.

Added to that, there wouldn't be time now to look in on the young mother who had been hurt in the car crash. Perhaps she would manage to go and look in on her later. In the meantime, she could have a word with the ward sister about her condition. She needed to know how she was progressing.

'What are you doing here? I thought this was supposed to be your day off?' A familiar, deep voice cut into her thoughts and she glanced up to see that Adam was coming towards her. She stopped, the sudden encounter making her heart begin to thump discordantly in her chest, sending the blood rushing to her head. She hadn't expected to run into Adam.

His stride was purposeful, and she guessed that he was heading towards A and E. Perhaps he had just come out from one of the offices along here.

He looked immaculate in a dark grey suit, the jacket sitting well on his broad shoulders, the perfect fit of his trousers drawing her attention to his long, muscular legs. He had caught up with her now, and his nearness sent her already overwrought nervous system into hyperdrive. He was altogether too male for her peace of mind, and memories of the closeness they had shared made her cheeks flush with heat.

He was waiting for an answer, and she managed to find her voice and said, 'Yes, this is my day off, but I've just been up to the wards to visit my neighbour, Dean. I treated him when he took too many painkilling tablets and ended up in here.' She turned with him into another corridor and they walked together towards the next junction.

Adam nodded. 'I remember. It happened on your first day at work, didn't it? How's he doing?'

'He's a lot better. The knee has healed up nicely, too, but he'll need some intensive physiotherapy to get him moving properly again. At the moment he's hobbling about on crutches.'

'That's good, isn't it…that he's up and about, I mean? So, when will he be going home? I would have thought it would be any day now if he's on his feet.'

'You're right. He was hoping to go home soon, but the doctor wanted to make sure that he would be able to get around at the flat before he agreed to it. I said I'd keep an eye on him whenever I was home and they're going to arrange some transport for him for when they finally agree to release him.'

Hannah glanced along the corridor and came to a

halt. 'I'm heading for the café to meet up with Abby and Ellie…that's another neighbour…and her little girl. We were planning on having a day out on the river.'

'That sounds as if it will be fun.' He sent her a quizzical glance. 'I suppose Ryan is going along on this trip with you?'

She shook her head. 'He's travelling back to the Chilterns to visit our foster-parents.' Her expression sobered.

'Oh, I see.' He frowned. 'You look as though that bothers you. Is something wrong? Are you sorry he's not still with you?'

'No. He only planned on staying with me for a day or so.' She wasn't going to share her worries about her foster-brother with Adam, but the truth was it troubled her that Ryan had not managed to sort out his problems with his landlord and that the debt collectors were still hot on his heels.

Adam was watching her curiously, as though he would have probed further, but instead he murmured, 'I imagine it's good that he's going back for a visit. Does your adoptive mother manage to keep in touch with all the children who have been in her care? There must have been quite a number over the years.'

'She's stayed in contact with all of them, but I think Ryan and I were with her for longer than the other children, and of course she adopted me in the end. She tells all the foster-children that she wants them to think of her house as home. That's how it was. She made us feel as though we belonged with her. She says we're all part of her big family.'

'A woman with a heart of gold, then?'

Hannah's lips curved as memories of happier times flooded through her. 'You could say that.'

Adam was looking at her oddly, and she tilted her head slightly as she studied him. 'What's wrong?'

'Nothing.' He shook his head. 'I haven't seen you smile like that in a long time.'

'No? Well, Mum is someone special. She's had to deal with all sorts of children over the years, children who were coping with problems of separation and those from all kinds of troubled backgrounds, but somehow she manages to bring out the best in everyone.'

'That can't have been easy for her. It takes a special kind of person to be able to do that.'

'Yes, it does.' She locked those thoughts inside herself and said quietly, 'Do you know if there has been any news of the woman we brought in the other day… Jessica, the young mother with the aortic rupture? I heard that she came through the operation, but that she had been taken to Intensive Care. No one could tell me any more when I enquired after her, and I've been worrying ever since…I keep seeing her little girl in my mind.'

'I heard just a short time ago that the surgery was successful and that she's making a good recovery. They're keeping her under observation, but I think she'll do just fine.'

Hannah let out a slow breath. 'I'm so relieved. I was afraid that there might be some nasty complications.'

'That was always on the cards, but our thoracic surgeon is exceptionally skilled, and he tried out a fairly new technique. He sealed the injury with a stent graft to control the haemorrhage. Instead of doing major surgery, he inserted an introducer sheath into the femoral artery and pushed the self-expanding stent into place using a special device. Doing things this new way means that there's minimal surgical damage, and it has a good success rate.'

'She's been fortunate, then, in a way?'

'You could say that.' He sent her a quick glance, his gaze flicking over her and taking in her soft cotton top and the skirt that clung to her hips and kicked out in a gentle swirl below her knees. 'But it was thanks to your careful observation that she survived at all. You should be pleased with yourself.'

It was strong praise, coming from him, and warm colour tinged her cheeks. 'I was anxious for her. It was instinct, really.'

'Maybe.' He looked thoughtful, but his grey eyes gave nothing away.

'I should go,' she said. 'Abby and Ellie will be waiting for me.'

'I won't keep you, then.' His searching gaze made her uncomfortably aware of the simplicity of her summer outfit. It wasn't anything special, and she wished she knew what he was thinking. Only the light jacket she was wearing was the same one that she had worn when Ryan had come with her the other day to A and E. Had he noticed that? Had it stirred memories in him? It shouldn't disturb her after all this time, should it? There was always going to be a barrier between him and Ryan.

He watched her turn to go on her way, and as she walked away from him she felt the heat of his gaze on the back of her neck. It didn't mean anything, of course, that he was keeping his attention fixed on her. It was more than likely that he was simply remembering her connection with Ryan, and was questioning whether he had seen the last of him.

She went to meet up with Abby and Ellie, who was brimming over with excitement at the thought of the trip that lay ahead. 'Is we going on a big boat?' she asked, her eyes wide, then added in a sudden afterthought, 'What if I fall in the water?'

'We're not going to let you fall in,' Abby said, chuckling. 'You'll be quite safe, I promise.'

They boarded the boat at Westminster Pier, and stood on deck, watching the waters of the Thames and the riverside scenery, as they cruised along by the South Bank.

The sun was a shimmering, golden globe, and there was only a faint breeze, making it ideal for their day out. Abby stood against the boat rail, looking out over the water, and said thoughtfully, 'I meant to ask you how your foster-brother's day out went. Did he go and visit the woods?'

'Yes, he did. He said they were well worth seeing. He even jotted down some notes and made a few quick sketches. He showed them to me, and they're really good. He's quite artistic, but he doesn't often put his talent into practice.'

'I'm glad it worked out for him. He seemed a bit down when I talked to him.'

Hannah nodded. 'Yes, I noticed that, too. I think he

was a little brighter in himself when he came home, though.' Ryan still hadn't told her any more about why he was in debt, or how the damage to his accommodation had been caused, and she worried about that. She had believed that he had put his rebellious years behind him and she had faith in him that he had changed for the better. Even so, she wished she knew what was going on.

She glanced at Abby. 'What about you? Are you all right? You don't seem to be your usual self today.'

'I'm fine, I think. It's probably just that I'm fighting off a virus of some sort. I've been a bit headachy lately, but I expect it's just a cold coming on. That's why I didn't go with you to see Dean earlier today. I thought if I had a coffee and a couple of paracetamol I would start to feel better.'

'I'm sorry.' Hannah was dismayed. 'We could have done this another day, you know, if you're not feeling well.'

Abby smiled. 'No, I wanted to come out today, rather than be stuck at home in the flat, and I didn't want to let Ellie down. She's been talking about this trip all week.'

Ellie started waving a hand in the air. 'What's that?' she said, pointing to a place on the riverside. The huge circle of the London Eye rose up against the blue backcloth of cloudless sky, and Abby hugged her and explained what it was, pointing out the glass capsules where people stood and looked out at the view over the city.

'We'll have a ride on it one day,' Abby promised.

Ellie nodded, looking pleased about that, and then

pointed a finger towards the London Aquarium building. 'We been there,' she said gently. Then she frowned. 'I didn't like the big fish. They was big as this…'

She spread her arms wide to show her, and Hannah laughed. 'It's a good thing they were in a huge tank, then.'

Their journey took them past the Tower of London and the remarkable sight of the Millennium Dome before they started back towards Westminster Pier.

Ellie was enthralled by her sightseeing cruise. 'Can we go on the boat again another day?' she asked, when they were back on dry land some time later. They started to walk towards the nearest tube station.

'Yes, I expect so,' Abby told her. 'You had a good time, then?'

Ellie nodded vigorously. 'I liked seeing the ducks,' she said. 'They was the bestest.'

Hannah and Abby exchanged wry looks. 'We could have taken her to the park, if that was all she wanted,' Abby murmured ruefully.

Hannah smiled, and glanced at her friend. 'Are you feeling worse?' she asked. 'You're looking a bit off colour.'

'I don't feel too good,' Abby admitted, 'and my headache's really bad now. I'm not sure quite what's brought it on, because I've had a lovely, restful day.'

'Perhaps we should go and sit down somewhere for a while?'

'That's probably a good idea.'

By the time they reached a café, though, Abby had

taken a turn for the worse, and Hannah was beginning to be really worried about her. Her friend was feverish, and some of what she was saying was starting to make no sense at all. Hannah sat her down on a bench seat, and Abby slumped sideways.

'Why isn't Mummy talking to me any more?' Ellie asked. 'Is she poorly?'

'Yes, Ellie. She's very poorly. I think we need to get someone to help us to look after her.'

Hannah checked Abby's pulse. It was lower than it should be, and her consciousness was slipping. From the look of her, this was more than just a simple viral infection.

Hannah took out her phone and called for an ambulance. 'I'm going to try and get your mummy to hospital,' she told Ellie. 'The doctors and nurses will be able to look after her there, and they'll try to make her well again.'

Ellie was unusually quiet. Abby's skin was hot to the touch, and Hannah tried to cool her down by drenching a handkerchief in cold, bottled water and applying it to her brow. It didn't seem to be having much effect.

By the time the ambulance came, Abby was starting to convulse. Hannah shielded her from Ellie so that the child would not be upset any more than was necessary, and once they were in the ambulance, Hannah tended to her friend.

'Will you let A and E know that there are signs of raised intracranial pressure?' she asked the paramedic. 'I'm very worried about her. I think we'll need to do a CT scan.'

'I'll do that,' the paramedic said. 'We'll get her to hospital as soon as possible.'

Adam met her in the ambulance bay. As soon as he had made a swift examination, he instructed his team to take Abby for a scan and electroencephalogram. 'You should stay back,' he told Hannah. 'Let us deal with her.'

'But she's my friend,' Hannah protested. 'I want to do something for her.'

'I know you do, but perhaps you should stay and take care of the little girl for a while. She must be confused enough as it is.'

He was right, of course, and Hannah put an arm around Ellie and led her away. She was shocked and upset by the way things had turned out, but she had to be strong for the child's sake.

'What's wrong with my mummy?' Ellie asked again.

'I don't know, sweetheart. The doctor will come and tell us as soon as he's taken care of her.' She turned the child towards the doctors' lounge. 'We'll go to the room where the doctors have their coffee-breaks,' she told her. 'There's a table in there, and you can sit and draw for a while.' She might even be able to borrow some toys from one of the waiting rooms. They would help to take Ellie's mind off things for a time.

When they reached the lounge, she settled Ellie by the table. 'Would you like some ice cream? I think there might be some in our fridge.'

Ellie nodded, but didn't say anything more. She sat and drew pictures on paper that Hannah found for her and played with the toys, and Hannah waited for news.

It was a long time coming. Eventually, Adam came into the room and said quietly, 'We're going to admit her. We've done a lumbar puncture and taken throat swabs so that we can be clearer as to what's happening. I suspect that the inflammation of her brain is being caused by a viral infection, so we're treating that with an infusion of an antiviral drug, acyclovir, along with mannitol to minimise the swelling of the brain tissues. It's too early to see results just yet, but there hasn't been any change for the worse, and that's something to be thankful for.'

Hannah nodded. 'Thank you for taking care of her. Can I go up and see her?'

'You can, but she's still not very responsive and she needs to rest. Make it a quick visit.'

'I will. I think it might help Ellie if she can see her mother for a moment or two before I take her home.'

'Are you going to take her to stay with her grandparents?'

Hannah shook her head. 'I don't know where they are. They haven't been in touch with Abby over the last few years, and they've never met Ellie. I'll try to find them, but in the meantime Ellie can stay with me. It will be less disorientating for her that way.'

'Are you sure that's wise?' Adam said in a low voice. 'Don't you think you have enough to cope with already?'

'I don't see that I have any choice. Abby is my friend, and I know that she wouldn't want Ellie to go to strangers. I'll have to find a childminder who can take care of her while I'm at work.'

'How will you do that?'

Hannah shrugged. 'Perhaps one of Abby's friends will be able to help out. I'll ask around at the nursery school.'

'Well, whatever you decide, I'll see you both home. I'm due to finish my shift here now, and when you come back down from the ward, I'll have my car outside, waiting.'

'You don't have to do that…'

'I know I don't, but I've made up my mind, so don't argue with me, Hannah. I think you've both had enough for one day, and Ellie looks wiped out.'

He was as good as his word. When Hannah came back from seeing Abby, he helped her and Ellie into his gleaming silver car and made sure that Ellie was fastened into a child seat.

'Where did that come from?' Hannah asked, frowning.

'I bought it for my brother,' he explained. 'He's expecting a new addition to his family in a month or so. This gift is a bit premature, but you know my family, we all like to plan ahead.'

She managed a faint smile. His was a strong family unit. They were all well-grounded, confident, successful people. Even thinking about them made her feel inadequate.

When they drew up outside the house just a short time later, she had something new to worry about. What would he think of her tiny flat? He was used to the very best and his father's estate covered acres of ground. He was almost bound to suffer from culture shock when he saw her place, wasn't he? Perhaps she was worrying unnecessarily, though. He might not want to waste time coming into the house.

'It looks as though Ellie's half-asleep already,' he said as he switched off the ignition and looked at the small child in the back seat. 'I'll carry her inside for you.'

'Thanks. I'll put her straight to bed,' Hannah murmured. It seemed as though her hope that he might stay away was dashed.

She led the way up to her flat. 'It isn't up to much in here,' she warned him, 'but it's easy to clean and the furniture is reasonably good quality.'

He settled Ellie down on the bed, and then looked around. 'Where is she going to sleep?' he asked. 'There's only one bed, and that's a single.'

'She can stay there. I'll make up the sofa bed for myself.'

'Do you have a bathroom, or do you have to share with the other tenants?' He was frowning.

'No, I have my own bathroom. It's through there.' She waved a hand towards a door. 'There's a shower, but it isn't actually working at the moment.' She grimaced.

'What's wrong with it?'

'I'm not sure… Someone came to fix another plumbing problem, and now I can't get the shower to come on. I'll have a word with the landlord about it as soon as he returns from his holiday.'

Adam raised a brow. 'When's that going to be?'

'Around three weeks' time, I think. He was going to cruise the Greek islands. Lucky for some.' She attempted a smile, but in fact none of this seemed real, or relevant, while her friend was ill in hospital. This whole business was unsettling her. How was she going to cope with looking after Ellie?

'Would you like a hot drink?' she asked. 'I can make tea or coffee…and perhaps a sandwich, if you like?'

She thought he would probably refuse, but he said, 'That would be great, thanks. Tea and a sandwich would be good. I haven't eaten for a while.'

Before she did that, she went to cover Ellie with a light duvet. The child was drowsy, but stirred enough to ask, 'When's my mummy coming home?'

'I don't know, sweetheart. I hope she'll be well again soon, but until then you can stay here with me. I'll look after you. I'll get hold of the key to your mummy's flat and bring some of your toys up here.' She stroked the little girl's curls and tried to soothe her. She would need to bring a supply of clothes, too.

Ellie was frowning, staring into space. 'I want my mummy,' she said.

'I know.'

Hannah tucked the teddy bear under the duvet so that Ellie could cuddle him, and then she sat on the edge of the bed, gently comforting her until the child's eyelids began to droop. She knew only too well what Ellie must be going through, being separated from her mother.

When she finally stood up, she saw that Adam was across the room in the annexe that was her small kitchen, making tea. She pulled the screen she had bought around the bed, dimmed the light and went to help him with the preparations for supper.

He had already started making the sandwiches, and she said awkwardly, 'Sorry, I didn't mean for you to have to do that. I hadn't expected to take so long. She was half-awake, and she was feeling anxious.'

He nodded. 'I heard what she was saying.' He sent her an oblique glance and said, 'You look uneasy. Everything that's happened must have been upsetting for you.'

She poured the tea, and said quietly, 'I'm worried about Abby… She looked in a bad way when I left her, and I can imagine how bewildered Ellie must be feeling right now.'

He pushed a plate of sandwiches towards her. He had found cheese, ham and salad in her fridge, and he had made up a selection. 'I suppose you've been through all that yourself…not once, but many times. This must have brought it all back to you.'

She nodded. 'Just lately, it doesn't take much for the memories to come flooding back. I remember being moved from pillar to post, finding myself in different foster-homes from time to time, wondering when I was going to see my mother again.' She sent him a swift glance. 'Shall we take these into the sitting room? We can at least sit down in there.'

'If you like.' Adam loaded up a tray with cups and plates and carried everything through to the main room, setting the tray down on a low coffee-table. They sat on the sofa and Hannah sipped at her tea, feeling its warmth slowly revive her.

'Didn't your father ever look after you when your mother wasn't around?' he asked. 'I know he was asked once, but he had only just remarried then. What about later on?' He bit into his sandwich, waiting for her answer.

'He did, for a short time, when my mother was taken ill. He persuaded his wife to have me stay with them for a while, but they had a child of their own by then, and it didn't really work out. I went back to my mother for a while, but soon after that she had a nervous breakdown. I had the feeling that my mother was unhappy because he had married someone else. It wasn't long after that when I went into long-term foster-care.'

'It must have been very confusing for you. It's almost as though your mother tried her best, but wasn't able to cope.'

'I suppose so.' She was quiet for a moment or two, thinking about that. 'I've come to the stage, now, where I need answers, once and for all, even if I'm not going to like what I find.'

'Have you had any success in searching for your mother?' he asked.

She shook her head. 'The missing persons line hasn't come up with anything yet, and I've tried an internet search. There have been a few false leads… I followed up on one or two, but either the people were the wrong age or they didn't fit the description properly.'

'That must have been a blow?'

She nodded. 'Yes, it was. I should have been prepared for disappointment, but I was so hopeful when the information came through. Someone had discovered where my grandmother used to live, and I rushed to check it out, but it turned out to be a wasted journey. My grandmother passed on some years ago, and the house was sold. There are strangers living there now.'

Her fingers fidgeted in her lap. 'I don't appear to have

any other relatives, but I suppose I just have to keep on looking. I'm searching the local records offices, just now, looking for any mention of my mother or her family.'

Her mouth made a straight line. 'At least, I can be fairly certain that my mother wasn't in trouble with the police, or involved with drugs or alcohol, and I'm thankful for that—I feel so sorry for Ryan, because he knows his background, and there's nothing he can do but live with it. I think it colours everything he does, and that's why he was in trouble such a lot when he was younger. He was even more disturbed than I was.'

'You can't compare yourself with Ryan.' His tone was dismissive. 'He had a choice, the same as you did. He decided to kick against the system, and cause mayhem, whereas you made something of your life… You made up your mind to become a doctor, and you worked hard until you had carried that ambition through. You can be proud of yourself.'

She looked at him. 'I don't feel that way. I feel as though I'm out of place, at odds with everything. I want answers to questions that go way back.'

'Hasn't it helped you to know that your adoptive mother cares about you…loves you? Her feelings towards you are genuine, I'm sure.'

'I know that, and I love her dearly, too, and I'll always be thankful that she took me in and treated me like her own child. Even so, I was with my natural mother on and off for the first years of my life, and I can't help feeling as though there's this huge, empty space inside me. My life is a jigsaw with pieces missing, and until I've found them I shan't be complete.'

Adam's arm went around her. 'I know that all this must be difficult for you, but I can't help thinking that you might come to regret looking for your mother in the end. You don't know what you're going to uncover, and the answers to your questions might make you feel worse than you do already.'

'Even so, I don't think I can move on until I know the truth of what happened…of why my mother left. If she had been ill, why didn't she come back for me when she recovered? I feel as though I'm stuck in some other dimension, as though my life's on hold.'

He drew her close to him, and she registered the warmth of his embrace just as if he had folded a warm blanket around her, sheltering her from a cold, harsh wind.

'I wish I could take some of the hurt away from you,' he murmured, his voice softening, his grey gaze moving over her with slow deliberation, smoothing over her like a balm to her shattered senses.

He leaned towards her, his long body gently pressuring hers, urging her to nestle up against him. She could feel the steady beat of his heart beneath her cheek, and she lifted her gaze to him. Then, slowly, compellingly, his head lowered and his mouth claimed the softness of her lips.

It was a gentle, explorative brush of his mouth on hers, and then he lightly nudged her lips apart. She was suddenly dizzy with the shocking, unexpected intimacy of that kiss, her body vibrant with smouldering sensation that sparked into white-hot flame.

He tasted the fullness of her lips, the sweetness of her mouth, and his kiss was slow and tender, his tongue lightly flicking along the lush curves, coaxing a sizzling, sensual response from her.

Hannah's head was spinning. She couldn't resist that honeyed invitation, but neither was she prepared for the way her treacherous body was reacting to him, for the way her senses erupted into tumultuous disorder. All at once, this wasn't enough. She wanted so much more.

He seemed to recognise that urgent need in her. His hands swept over her, inciting an urgent thrill of sensation to ripple through her body, filling her with unbidden, tantalising hunger for something she couldn't define.

'You take my breath away,' he said, in a low ragged voice. His glance trailed over her like the lick of flame, and his grey eyes became smoky with desire as his fingers slid along the line of her bare arm, smoothing over the silk of her skin.

The tender brush of his hands over her soft curves made her pulses leap, and she melted against him, her softly feminine curves merging with the powerful, muscled strength of his body.

Wasn't this what she had always wanted, longed for? For so many years, she had watched Adam from afar, respected him, idolised him, had dared to believe that he might be the one man who had the power to make her whole again, and yet her dreams had ultimately been shattered.

Ellie began to stir, mumbling in her sleep, a sob in her voice. Hannah swallowed, coming to her senses slowly, and perhaps Adam recognised her withdrawal from him, because he looked at her quizzically.

'Hannah?'

She couldn't answer that unspoken question. He wouldn't understand.

Perhaps she had been fooling herself all along. He lived in a different world from hers and the two would never come together, would they? Besides, she couldn't rely on him to be there for her, fighting her corner. Where had he been when she had needed him to support Ryan's cause?

She had been desolate when her mother had left her behind, but it had made her fiercely protective of those who were dear to her. Ryan had always been her ally, her defender, like the brother she had never had, and she would never let him down by going over to the enemy.

Hannah said softly, 'I should go and check on Ellie. She's going to be unsettled for quite a while, as long as her mother is away from her.'

'Yes, that's probably true.' Adam had never really taken to Ryan, and then he had made his position clear by siding with his father and hurting her foster-brother in the process.

He was watching her carefully. 'Hannah…about what just happened…between you and me…'

'It was a mistake,' Hannah cut in. 'Perhaps we should put it behind us. It's been a long day for both of us, and I, for one, wasn't thinking too clearly.'

He nodded and seemed to brace himself. 'You're right. Anyway, I'd better go. As you say, it's been a long and difficult day. We should forget what happened this evening. We have to work together, and it wouldn't do for us to let any relationship get in the way.' He stood up. 'I'll see myself out. You should go and see to Ellie.'

She didn't look at him as he left the room. She was afraid that her face would betray her feelings, and she felt extraordinarily close to tears.

CHAPTER SIX

'I'M WORRIED about Ryan.' Hannah's adoptive mother sounded distracted on the phone, as though she was making the call while she was on the move. 'I was talking to one of his friends, and he let slip that Ryan was having problems with his tutor. It sounds as though he was being hostile and argumentative, and the tutor was threatening to throw him off his course, but the friend wouldn't tell me any more. Do you know what's going on, Hannah?'

'This is the first I've heard of it,' Hannah admitted. It didn't sound like the Ryan she knew, but it worried her all the same. 'It might just be the pressure of exams,' she said, searching for a reason. 'Anyway, I'll try to get in touch with him and find out more, but I don't know how much he'll tell me. Whatever the outcome, I'll do my best to help him out, I promise.'

'Thanks, Hannah, I knew I could rely on you. I must go. I have to take the dog to the vet for his booster injection. You know how difficult that's going to be. Saxon hates going in the car.'

Hannah laughed. 'I remember… A bit of bribery's

called for…a few biscuits or treats strategically placed on the back seat might do the trick. Best of luck. Bye, Mum. I'll talk to you later.'

Hannah cut the call, and walked from the inner courtyard, where she had been taking a quick afternoon break, back into A and E. She wasn't having a good day. All of her patients so far had been difficult to treat and had suffered complications, and Adam was watching her like a hawk. Now she had the added worry of wondering what was going on with Ryan.

'I see that you have your patient on a cardiac monitor,' Adam said when he found her studying some lab test results a few minutes later. 'Have you thought about the differential diagnosis?' His tone was brisk, and he seemed to be in a hurry, flicking casually through the patient's notes while he was on the move.

'Yes, I have, but I'm not convinced that there isn't a primary hyperparathyroidism.' Hannah stood her ground. He was putting her through a cross-examination, but she was sure of her facts and she didn't see why he would want to interfere with her treatment of this patient.

'She's lost weight, has generalised aches and pains, muscle weakness, thirst and excessive urination, and the blood tests have come back showing loss of magnesium and potassium and a high serum calcium. Given all her symptoms, I want to start her on fluids right away. I planned on rehydrating her with isotonic saline and 5 per cent dextrose, with potassium and magnesium supplements.'

'That will certainly help to lower the serum calcium.'

He glanced at the results. 'Give her a bisphosphonate in saline infusion over four hours. That will inhibit the resorption from bone.' He handed the chart back to her. 'You should get a parathyroid hormone measurement, and then you might need to refer her for surgery.'

'That's what I thought.'

He nodded. 'I'll leave it with you, then. If there are any problems, ask Colin to give you a hand, or give Mr Tremayne a call. I'll be in a meeting in the personnel office for the next half-hour or so.'

He walked away from her, and she watched him go, unsure what to make of his manner. He was being utterly businesslike, and she didn't know how to take his cool, matter-of-fact approach to her. It felt as though he was distancing himself from her, and perhaps she only had herself to blame for that.

'He's going for a meeting about the consultant's post,' Colin said, coming to stand alongside her and following Adam's progress along the corridor. 'Mr Tremayne looks set to move on in a couple of months, and Adam is the most likely candidate for the job.'

'I didn't know it was being sorted out just yet,' Hannah said. The news had a dampening effect on her, but it shouldn't have come as a surprise. Of course he would want to stay in London…he thrived on city life, and he was more than ready for a consultant position. She hadn't ever really believed that he might eventually go back to the Chilterns to work, had she?

'I think this is just a preliminary stage, but the result is probably cut and dried. We all know that they'd have to be mad not to give it to Adam. He's a terrific doctor, he's good with the patients and when he's in charge everything runs smoothly.'

There was no denying that. The news had left her feeling strangely subdued, though, and added to his curt, challenging attitude towards her today, she was less than happy about the way things were going.

She went back to her patient and talked to Sarah about the infusion and the test results. Perhaps it was best not to think about what the future had in store. Her emotions were in a state of flux, and they were especially chaotic where Adam was concerned.

Some time later, her shift ended and she headed back to her flat, stopping off on the way to pick up Ellie from her childminder. As she had hoped, one of Abby's friends had agreed to help out.

Ellie was not in a happy mood. 'Why isn't Mummy fetching me?' she wanted to know.

'Because she's still very poorly,' Hannah told her gently. 'I explained it all to you, didn't I? She has to stay in hospital for a while.'

'Why?'

'So that the doctors can try to make her well again. I'm sure you'll be able to go and see her just as soon as she's feeling a bit better.'

Abby's condition was still giving cause for concern. The virus had caused swelling around her brain, and the medical team was doing everything that they possibly could for her. Hannah could only hope that she would recover without suffering any additional complications.

'We'll make pancakes when we get home,' Hannah told Ellie. 'You like those, don't you?'

'With syrup?' Ellie queried.

'Yes, with syrup,' Hannah agreed. 'Dean's home from hospital, and he's going to come and have supper with us, so we'd better make quite a few, hadn't we?'

Ellie nodded vigorously. 'Yum…mmm…' she said. Then she asked, 'Is his leg better?'

'Yes, I think so, but it's still a bit stiff, so he has to be careful how he gets about, and he's using an elbow crutch to help him along.'

Dean was hobbling about the place when they arrived home, and he came and joined them in Hannah's flat, helping her with the preparations for supper.

'How have you coped on your own all day?' Hannah asked, as they tucked into vegetable risotto. Ellie fed her doll with a plastic spoon and chatted to her throughout the meal, taking no notice of the adults at the table. 'Have you been able to get around all right?'

'It hasn't been too bad.' He grimaced. 'I'll be glad when I'm back to normal, though. I want to get on with my life and go back to work.'

'That's understandable.' Hannah finished off her first course and then put plates under the grill to warm. She spooned pancake mix into a hot pan and set it on the cooker to heat up once more. 'I heard that your parents were on their way over. Abby left them a message when you were taken into hospital, and I found their reply when I checked her answering-machine. They've been out of the country, but they should be here to see you tomorrow.'

Dean made a crooked smile. 'Really? I'd better clean the place up, then, or Mum will think I'm living in squalor and will want to be hauling me off back home. Do they know I'm out of hospital?'

'Yes, I phoned them.' She frowned. 'I wish it was as easy to get in touch with Abby's parents. I've spoken to the Salvation Army and they're going to see if they can find out where they are. They've never even met Ellie, but surely they'll want to come and see Abby if they know that she's ill?'

'Let's hope so.'

Between them, Dean and Ellie demolished the pile of pancakes that she made, and Hannah started to clear away the crockery. 'Will you watch Ellie for me while I wash up?' she asked Dean, and he nodded.

A few minutes later, as she was drying up and putting everything away, the doorbell rang, and Dean went to see who was there.

'Hello, Ellie,' she heard Adam say, and then he added, presumably to Dean, 'Is Hannah around?'

Dean pointed towards the kitchen, and Hannah came out into the main room. 'Adam,' she said, looking at him in surprise. 'I wasn't expecting to see you here. Is everything all right?' And then, her tone anxious, she went on, 'Nothing's happened to Abby, has it?'

He shook his head. 'No…as far as I know, she's still much as she was before.' He looked at her guardedly, his glance moving over her, taking in the light cotton top that she was wearing and gliding down over her snugly fitting blue jeans. 'I came about the shower. I suppose you're still having trouble with it?'

'Oh, I see…' She blinked. 'Yes, it's still not working.' She couldn't get her head around the fact that he was here at all. He was dressed in casual clothes, dark chinos and a matching top, and he looked incredibly good, so striking that her heart skipped a beat and she floundered for a moment or two. 'I've been managing by taking a shower at work or in Abby's flat,' she said.

'I had a word with someone who knows about these things,' he said. 'I thought, as Ellie's staying with you, you might need to get it fixed fairly quickly. Do you know where your mains tap is? Is it all right if I take a look?'

'Help yourself,' she said, still out of synch with what was going on, but waving him in the direction of the kitchen. 'It's in the kitchen cupboard, under the drainer.'

He took off his jacket and draped it over a chair, before going into the kitchen. A minute or so later, he went into the bathroom and examined the shower.

'That seems to be working all right now,' he said, after a while, drying his hands on a towel and coming back into the sitting room.

She stared at him, open-mouthed. 'It was as easy as that?' she asked. 'How did you do that?'

'The mains pressure was too low, and the safety cut-out pressure valve in the shower stops it from working. Hopefully, you won't have any problems from now on.'

She smiled at him. 'That's wonderful... Thank you. I had no idea it was so simple. I feel like such a fool.'

'You weren't to know.' He turned to Dean. 'How are you? You look better than you did last time I saw you.'

Hannah listened as they talked for a while, but her mind was stuck on the fact that Adam was there at all. A warm bubble of happiness rose inside her, until she remembered that, of course, he hadn't done any of this for her, had he? He said it was Ellie he had been thinking about. Disappointment washed through her and she had to make a conscious effort to tune back in to what was going on.

The doorbell rang again, and she frowned. Her small flat was seeing more visitors this evening than it had in all the time she'd been staying here. Going over to the door and pulling it open, she was startled to see Ryan waiting outside in the hallway.

'Ryan, this is lovely… I had no idea that you might be coming to see me.' Her face lit up in a smile, but at the same time she became aware of Adam stiffening. Uncertain how to handle things, she said, 'Ryan, I'm not sure if you know Dean. He lives in the flat across the hall… And you remember Ellie, don't you? Her mother's in hospital just now, so she's staying with me.' Briefly, she explained what had happened to Abby.

Ryan frowned, and Hannah went on, 'And Adam's only just arrived. He fixed my shower for me. I've been lost without it.'

Ryan acknowledged Dean and Ellie, and then glanced towards Adam. He said nothing, and Adam nodded in Ryan's direction. Hannah immediately felt awkward. What could she do to smooth things out between these two men?

'I've just made pancakes,' she said, 'and there are a couple left. Perhaps you and Adam might like to finish them off? They should still be warm from the grill.' She wasn't at all sure what her foster-brother was doing there. Had he come to stay again? How was she going to be able to ask him about his problems with his tutor with Adam and Dean in the room?

'I'll have something to eat, thanks, but I didn't plan on stopping for long,' Ryan said. 'I just thought I'd drop by on the off chance that you would be at home. I've come from my friend's house, and I want to travel back to college tonight. I have to sit an exam tomorrow afternoon and I still have some studying to do.' He hesitated. 'I might just pop in and see Abby if she's in the hospital, though, as I'm in the area. She was good to me and I don't like to think of her being alone and ill.'

'I'm sure she'll appreciate that. I don't know how responsive she'll be, though. She's on medication to bring down the inflammation around her brain, but it may not have calmed things down enough yet. I think she'll be glad to know that you stopped by, though.'

Ellie stared at Ryan. 'I seen you before,' she said. 'You was talking to my mummy. Mummy said you was in trouble.' She screwed up her face, as though she was trying to remember. 'She said you might have nowhere to live.'

Ryan almost choked on his pancake, and Hannah saw that Adam was frowning. Even so, he had the presence of mind to thump Ryan on the back to clear the obstruction from his throat, and Ryan recovered slowly, his eyes watering slightly. He still didn't acknowledge Adam.

'Is you all right?' Ellie watched what was going on, her eyes wide and fascinated.

'Yes, Ellie, I'm fine, thank you,' Ryan told her.

'Shall we go and look in your toy box, Ellie, and see what we can find?' Adam asked, taking her by the hand and leading her to a corner of the room. Perhaps he had decided to be diplomatic and pretend he hadn't taken any notice of what had been said.

'Why was he coughing?' Ellie asked. Hannah didn't hear Adam's reply, but she watched as he persuaded her to show him the contents of her toy box.

'I think it's time that I went back to my own flat,' Dean decided. 'I need to start cleaning up if my parents are coming to visit tomorrow.'

Hannah saw him out and then took Ryan to one side. 'Is it true, Ryan?' she asked in a low voice. She guessed that he wouldn't want Adam to hear what they were saying. 'Are you going to lose your accommodation? Haven't you been able to sort things out with your landlord? You know that you can stay here for a while if you want, if you're in trouble of any kind.'

'I haven't been thrown out yet. I'm still trying to get the money together to pay off the debts, and I missed out on a month's rent, that's all. The landlord's getting on my case, but I can't really blame him.' His tone was subdued and he turned away from where Ellie and Adam were checking out the animals in a Noah's Ark.

'I'll write you out a cheque,' she said softly. 'Let's get this sorted out once and for all.'

This time, he didn't refuse, and after he'd told her the amount, she wrote out a cheque and handed it to him. 'Is there anything else on your mind?' she asked, remembering what her mother had said earlier. 'Are you worried about the exams or your coursework?'

'No, not really. I had a bit of an argument with one of the tutors because I wanted some extra time to finish off a piece of work. He wouldn't give me any leeway, but I'm not too worried about the exams.'

'Have you managed to sort things out with your tutor?'

He grimaced. 'Not yet. He's a bit of a stuffed shirt, but I'll deal with it. I was only asking for a couple of days' grace. No one else has given us projects to finish this close to the exams and that's what I told him.'

'You'll tell me if there's anything else bothering you, won't you?'

'Of course.' He put an arm around her and smiled at her. 'You shouldn't worry. You're my best girl and I don't want you upset.'

Some time later, when he was ready to leave, she saw him out into the hallway. 'Good luck with the exams,' she said.

'Thanks.' He frowned. 'About the money...I'll pay you back just as soon as I can, I promise. It might take me a couple of months, though.'

'That's all right. Forget it. Just make sure you get it all sorted out.'

She watched him go and then went back inside the flat. Ellie was sitting in a chair with Adam, looking at the pictures in a book, and her eyelids were drooping.

'I should get her to bed,' Hannah said quietly. 'Thanks for watching over her.'

'She's a sweet child. It must be difficult for you, having to take care of her when you're not used to small children.' He frowned, looking unusually bewildered. 'They seem to have so much energy, and they ask so many questions…and every one seems to end with "why?".'

Hannah laughed. 'That's true enough. I've never worked out what the proper answer is to that one. Everything I say just leads to another "why?" and we sort of spiral downwards from there.'

Adam gently lifted Ellie from his lap and handed her over to Hannah. The child hardly stirred, and Hannah swiftly set about getting her ready for bed.

'It's been a long day for her,' she murmured, when she had at last settled her under the duvet. 'I expect she'll sleep like a log for the rest of the night.'

She put the screen in place and came back to the main part of the sitting room, glancing at Adam. 'Is your brother ready for his new addition to the family? He doesn't have any other children, does he?'

'No, this will be his first. I think he has everything in hand. He and his wife have just moved into a bigger house in Buckinghamshire and he's spending all his spare time getting the nursery ready for the baby.'

'It must be so lovely to be able to do that. Whenever Mum had a baby to look after, we had to shift everything about to make room. It was always chaos in our house. There were lots of rooms, but there never seemed to be enough space.'

He made a twisted smile. 'Perhaps there were just so many children about that you had trouble finding space to be yourself.'

'That's true.' She thought back over the chaos with affection. 'I wouldn't have liked to be without any of them, though.'

'No. I can see that you're still very attached to Ryan. He's more than a brother figure to you, isn't he? You're very close to one another. You worry about him and feel the need to look out for him.'

She lifted a brow. 'Is there something wrong with that?'

'Not at all…but I can't help thinking that he's all of twenty-five, twenty-six now, and I'm a little concerned that you should be placed in a position where you feel the need to bail him out with money for rent.'

Hannah winced. So he had seen and heard what was going on after all. 'I had hoped to be discreet about that,' she murmured. 'I suppose this place is just too small for anyone to have secrets.'

'Would you rather I pretended that I didn't know what was going on?' His expression was shuttered. 'What would be the point? I know that things are difficult for him right now, and that you want to help him. I just wonder if he might need to adjust his own attitude a little. After all, he mentioned that he was having trouble with his tutor, and I doubt that he'll be able to resolve anything if he's easily provoked, or if he allows his quick temper to get the better of him, as he did when he was younger.'

Her lips made an odd shape. 'Perhaps his tutor could do with a little more sensitivity in his approach. He should understand when a student is having problems and make an effort to ease back on the pressure he's bringing to bear on a situation.'

'Maybe.' Adam moved restlessly. 'You can't keep on protecting him for ever. There comes a time when everyone has to stand on their own two feet and deal with the consequences of their actions.'

'I wouldn't have expected you to understand,' Hannah said, her tone abrupt. 'Why would you? You and your family have always had everything going for you. You have wealth to smooth over any monetary problems and the back-up of a strong support network within your own family if ever there is trouble from outside.'

She pulled in a quick breath. 'You've never had to wonder where your parents might be, or whether you'll ever see them again, and you've never been moved from one place to another like an unwanted parcel. That's how it was for Ryan. Don't talk to me about standing on your own two feet. You've never had to stand alone and wonder where you were supposed to be or where you might finish up.' She glared at him.

'No, I haven't. You're right about that.'

He hesitated, and then started to walk towards the door. She frowned, following his progress, still heated from her defence of her brother. He turned at the door and said, 'I should go. Thanks for the food.'

He left the flat and was out of the building before she had time to come to her senses. When it dawned on her that he had actually gone, she felt waves of guilt wash over her.

What had she done? Why had she turned on him that way? He didn't deserve that after the way he had come to help her, did he?

Now she had alienated him, and she felt awful about that. How was she going to be able to mend her fences with him?

CHAPTER SEVEN

'WHY is your patient still here?' Adam frowned, flicking through the file with a hint of impatience. 'I thought you were making arrangements to admit him.'

'I'm still waiting for a bed to become available,' Hannah answered.

'Perhaps you should find somewhere else for him to stay while he's waiting. We need the treatment room.'

'I'm reluctant to move him just yet,' she said. She didn't want to go against Adam's orders, but instinct told her that all wasn't well with the man she was treating.

'What's the problem? Apart from the fact that you don't have all the test results back yet? He was brought in because of a high fever and pain in the right upper quadrant, wasn't he?' He checked her notes and added, 'You've managed to bring down his temperature, and you're giving him supportive treatment. I don't see any reason why he shouldn't be wheeled into a waiting area.'

'That's all true, but his pain level is getting worse despite the medication he's on, and I'm wondering if it's possible that he has a liver abscess.'

Adam looked sceptical. 'An abscess would be a relatively rare diagnosis.'

'Yes, I know.' She had been doubtful about putting forward the suggestion, but she had come this far and it would be an admission of defeat if she turned back now. She pulled in a quick breath and forged ahead, saying, 'Given the nature of the pain and the fact that there are signs of biliary disease, I want to at least rule it out. There could have been an obstruction that's caused infection to flare up, resulting in an abscess. I'd hate to leave it alone and then find that it has erupted and caused septicaemia.'

He studied her for a moment. 'Then you should do a CT scan.'

'Yes, that's what I planned to do.'

He nodded, and then moved away without commenting any further, and Hannah hesitated for a moment before going back to her patient. She hadn't seen Adam around the department for a day or two, and she guessed he must have been off duty.

Now that he was here, though, his manner towards her was coolly professional, nothing more, and that worried her. Was he still annoyed with her for the way she had turned on him the other day? She needed to put things right between them. It had been wrong of her to condemn him for his apparent dismissal of Ryan and his problems. He was at least entitled to express his opinion without having to fend off an attack from her about his way of life.

When she brought her patient back from having the CT scan, Adam was by the reception desk, going through the patients' charts, but he wasn't alone. His older brother, Taylor, was there with him, along with a young woman who appeared to be heavily pregnant. She guessed that she was his brother's wife.

Hannah acknowledged them with a nod, and wheeled her patient back into the treatment room. 'I'm going to leave you in the care of our nurse for a few minutes,' she told him, 'while I go and have a word with the registrar. I'll try not to be too long. I know that you're very uncomfortable.'

Her step faltered as she approached Adam and his brother. She had not seen much of Taylor when she had lived with her adoptive mother. He had often been away on business, but she guessed that he must at last be getting ready to put down roots now that they had a baby on the way.

Taylor was talking about the garden at his new property. 'We want to landscape it so that there's a child-friendly play area established by the time the baby is beginning to toddle around.' He laughed. 'Marianne has been busy buying every plant that catches her eye, but I keep telling her that we have to work out what's going where, depending on the soil type and whether a particular area gets the sun or whether it's in shade.'

Marianne shook her head. 'You have such a neat, tidy mind, don't you? I just know whether I like something or not, and I tell myself I'll decide where it's going to go when I get it home.' She smiled at him. 'Anyway, a lot of the plants were going cheap after the Chelsea Flower show, and I couldn't resist a bargain or two.'

'Or three, or four,' Taylor added, his mouth making a wry twist. He caught sight of Hannah and said, 'I know you, don't I? You're the girl from the house on

Calder Close, aren't you? Hannah, isn't it?' He frowned, trying to recall the memories. 'You used to come up to the estate sometimes.'

'I'm surprised that you remember me,' she said awkwardly. 'You weren't home very much, as I recall.'

'That's true, but I have a notion that I've seen you more than a few times over the years.' He introduced her to his wife, and said, 'We were just talking about getting the garden ready at our new house. Do you have a garden here in London, Hannah?'

She shook her head. 'I'm afraid I can't even manage a window-box in my tiny flat.' Her expression was wistful for a moment or two. 'I loved the garden back home, though. I miss it.'

Taylor nodded. 'Now I remember how it was…you were the quiet, shy one, weren't you? You loved being on the estate because it was so big and open, and you loved the fields and the stream. The last place you wanted to be was in the town or the city, with all the noise and the traffic. I remember you once said that you had travelled to London with your mother when you were a small child, and you didn't like it very much.'

He looked at her quizzically, in a way that reminded her very much of Adam's way of watching her. 'Do you still feel the same way, or are you planning to stay on in London? I'm assuming your post here is a temporary one, of course.'

'That's right, it is. I can't see myself staying on,' she admitted. 'I still prefer to live near the countryside. I thought I might try for a general practitioner position in a rural community, once I've completed my training.'

Adam's eyes narrowed on her, and he cut in, saying, 'Did you want something, Hannah? Is there a problem?'

'No problem,' she murmured, 'but I wondered if you would take a look at the CT film of Mr Nichols in treatment room three. I need a second opinion so that I know whether I should go ahead with the treatment.'

'Let's go and have a look.' He excused himself to his brother and Marianne, and went with her to look at the films.

'It certainly looks like an abscess,' he said a moment or two later. 'Have you had the rest of the results back from the lab yet?'

She nodded. 'The blood cultures were positive.'

'Hmm…then you should drain the abscess under ultrasound scanning and send a sample to the lab. The procedure should do something to relieve the pain, anyway. When you have the results, you might need to add another antibiotic to the metronidazole and ampicillin.'

'I'll go and prepare the patient for treatment now.' She paused, and as he would have turned to go back to his brother, she said quickly, 'I've been meaning to have a word with you all day. I wanted to say that I'm sorry for the way I let off steam the other day. I shouldn't have gone on at you the way I did, especially after you took the trouble to come and help me out with the shower.'

'You don't have to apologise. You said what you thought, and that's fine.'

'No, it isn't.' She moistened her lower lip with her tongue. 'I was out of order.'

'Go and treat your patient, Hannah. He needs your attention.'

She was crushed by his response. He wasn't going to let her put things right, was he? And now she felt worse than ever.

He was suddenly thoughtful. 'Have you aspirated a liver abscess before?' he asked.

She shook her head.

'Then I'll come and supervise.'

'Are you sure? What about your brother and his wife? You're on a break, aren't you?'

'I'll catch up with them later. They're going to be in the area for a few days. Just give me a minute to have a word with them. In the meantime, you could start getting your patient ready for the procedure.'

'I'll do that.' She didn't know what had prompted his decision. After all, she could have asked Colin to supervise, but perhaps Adam wanted to see for himself that all was being done correctly.

It was some time later when she was satisfied that she had done all she could for her patient. Adam had taken her through the process step by step, making sure that she accessed the abscess at the right angle and ensuring that all went smoothly.

'You did well to pick up on that diagnosis,' he said, when she had finished and was ready to move on.

She glanced at him. 'Thanks. I thought you were doubtful about it earlier on.'

'I was, but you argued your point, and it just goes to show that you're beginning to have more confidence in yourself. You carried through on your instinct, despite opposition, and that can only be good.'

'Maybe.'

'Definitely.' He made a fleeting smile. 'I think there's still one other difficulty you have that we ought to address, though.'

Her eyes widened a fraction. 'Really? What's that?'

'Your negative attitude towards the city. We need general practitioners here in the city just as much as we need them in rural areas, you know. Besides, if you find that your natural mother is living here, you might feel that you need to adjust your plans. I really think you need to get around and see the sights. You haven't given the city a proper chance.'

'I went on the river the other day,' she pointed out.

'That's not enough, by a long way. You should see the rest of the city, the green areas, the parks, the places where you can relax and simply enjoy nature. It might give you a different perspective on city life.'

'Perhaps I will, one day, when I have the time.'

He raised a dark brow. 'What's that supposed to mean?'

'It means that the only time I have to do any exploring is on my days off, and that's when I catch up on my chores, usually. Quite apart from the fact that I'm looking after Ellie these days, and a lot of time is spent taking her to see her mother in hospital.'

'Hmm… I can see that would be a problem. Then we'll just have to make a start today.' He sent her an oblique glance. 'You haven't had your lunch break yet, have you?'

She shook her head. 'Not yet.' She forestalled him. 'I have plans for my break. This afternoon is one of my study-break periods and I need to catch up on some of my paperwork.'

'That's even better,' he said with marked satisfaction. 'My shift finishes in a while, and I'm not on call until later in the afternoon, so we can both forget the paperwork for a time. Instead you can spend an hour or so in the city with me, studying the opportunities that are available for GPs who choose to work here.'

'Adam, I can't do that. You don't understand… I've a mountain of work to wade through…'

'I doubt that. You've always been an organised, conscientious woman, and you don't allow yourself to become so swamped with work that you're overwhelmed.'

She opened her mouth to say something, but floundered, like a fish out of water. How was it that he knew her so well? She frowned, sending him a bewildered, blue gaze.

'Today, the paperwork gets pushed to one side. We'll go out and get a leisurely lunch, somewhere where we can enjoy looking out onto a pleasant, open scene. Perhaps we'll take a walk in one of the parks.' Just in case she came up with any argument to the contrary, he added, 'You're coming with me, and that's final.' He sent her a sideways look. 'Anyway, you owe me…for the shower.'

'That was a low blow.' Her lips pursed.

'Yes, it was, wasn't it?' He looked pleased with himself and laughed. 'I'll meet up with you in half an hour.'

She thought about backing out at the last minute, but as she stood by the exit doors just a little later, she looked around her and saw that the sun was shining. It was inviting and she relaxed for a moment or two, pausing to drink in its warmth and let it bathe her in its golden glow.

Adam caught up with her. 'Hyde Park is probably the nearest,' he said, 'so perhaps we should head over there. His hand lightly rested on her elbow as he urged her towards the main thoroughfare and away from the hospital. 'You weren't thinking of skipping out on me, were you, by any chance?'

'Would I do that?' she asked, and was treated to a dubious stare. All at once, though, she was glad of the chance to spend some time with him, away from the hospital, away from the worries of looking after Ellie and all the demands that were being made of her. As he'd said, she owed him for the shower and perhaps this would make up for her ill-timed words afterwards.

They walked through tree-lined squares until they reached the Bayswater Road and then they turned onto the leafy North Carriage Drive. 'We'll head towards the Serpentine,' he said. 'We can eat at a restaurant over-looking the lake and watch the people out on the boats. It's warm enough for us to sit and have our meal outside if we can get a table.'

He led the way to the restaurant where they found a place to sit on a large terrace overlooking a garden area, and Hannah gazed around her, taking in the gentle chatter of people feeding ducks on the lake and the shouts of children running across the grass. For the first time in days, she gradually began to relax.

Their food was brought to their table, an appetising mix of meats and salad and sun-dried tomatoes. There was a dish of pasta, drizzled with a colourful, mouth-watering sauce, and a chilled wine to wash it all down.

'Feeling better?' Adam asked, as she laid down her fork and glanced around.

'Much better, thanks,' she murmured. She glanced up at him. 'How did you know? I haven't said that anything was wrong.'

'You didn't have to. I know you well enough to know that you've been feeling uptight these last few weeks. I thought perhaps it was because you were trying to adjust to life in the city, but I know there must be other things that are piling on the pressure…like worrying about Abby, not being able to find your mother, wondering what's going on with Ryan.'

'I hadn't realised that you'd even given it a thought,' Hannah said quietly. She took a sip of her wine, feeling its coolness slide down her throat and allay the heat of the day. The sky was a beautiful eggshell blue, and there was barely a cloud in sight. 'Of course, you didn't mention the difficulties of getting to grips with work in A and E.'

'I took that as read. After seeing your reaction to the flight in the air ambulance, I guessed the worst was nearly over. I thought after that you'd be able to handle just about anything.'

He chuckled, and speared a forkful of pasta, twisting it gently in the succulent vegetable sauce.

'I suppose I am a little more confident in what I do. It's been good, having you help me out and point me in the right direction, though you have been a bit exacting at times.'

He lifted a dark brow. 'You must have me confused with someone else.'

She shook her head. 'You thrive on all this, don't you…the city life, the adrenaline punch of emergency work?'

'It's never going to be an easy job, I accept that, but, yes, I'm comfortable with what I do, and I like living in London.'

The waitress came and cleared away their plates, and he gave her their order for dessert.

After she had gone, he said, 'When I was a young boy, my father used to bring me with him sometimes when he had to come to London on business, and I feel the same way about it as he does. The city can be an exciting place, full of opportunity. I don't really miss my country roots as you do. I was happy living on the estate back home, but I enjoy being in the city.'

'And this is where you plan to go on working as a consultant, isn't it? I heard that Mr Tremayne was leaving.'

She leaned back in her seat as the waitress brought their dessert, a confection of fresh fruit and ice cream laid out on a bed of melt-in-the-mouth pastry.

'It's a wonderful opportunity for me, to be offered promotion. It's been a good experience, working in a large teaching hospital, and a job as consultant would be the icing on the cake. It could be a stepping stone to even greater things…a lecture consultancy perhaps, in years to come.'

'I can see you doing that.' Even now, he was thinking ahead, ambitious for what was still out there.

She slid a spoon into her dessert and let the sweet, delicate flavours of the fruit burst on her tongue. It should have been a luscious, stimulating experience, but the taste turned to blandness in her mouth. Why was she forever looking for something more from Adam? He was going to stay here. He wasn't ever going to be content to go back home to the Chilterns. She had known that, but at the back of her mind, despite all their troubled background, she had wondered…had dared to hope that he might change his plans.

Ever since she had first known him, she had found him irresistible, and she had never quite managed to quell that unbidden, treacherous tug of desire. Nothing would come of it, though. It wouldn't do to think that way about him, would it?

'I suppose Ryan will be hoping to find work when his exams are over…is he looking for work in a particular area?'

'He hasn't said much about it, but I imagine that since he wants to keep his accommodation, he must be thinking of finding something locally. I hope it works out for him. I know he's been studying hard, despite all the setbacks he's had lately.'

If Adam thought that the setbacks were of Ryan's own making, at least he kept quiet about it. He said, 'Does he ever see his parents these days? I know he used to keep in touch with them from time to time.'

'I think he does. They were very young when they got together, and I don't think they were mature enough to cope with bringing up a child. Then there were problems with drugs and alcohol, and Ryan was eventually taken into care. Over the years, his mother has made an effort to get back on her feet, and Ryan goes to visit her from time to time. I think, like me, he needed to come to terms with his past.'

'Have you made any headway doing that? You said you had posted something on the internet. Have you had any luck so far?'

'Nothing, as yet. Someone contacted me to say that they used to live near my grandmother, but after she died the house was sold to pay off debts. Apparently, my mother only lived there for a short time. She moved on, and there was no forwarding address.'

'I'm sorry. That must have been hard for you.'

She pressed her lips together. 'I'm getting used to it. I tend not to get my hopes up now. I know that these leads might not go anywhere, but my foster-mother said that my mother came to London, and that was when she lost touch with her. We relied on the adoption agency to keep the details up to date, but either they lost her address or my mother moved house and didn't update them.'

'Has it occurred to you that she might not want you to contact her?'

'Yes, I've thought of that…but she had always tried to keep in touch before then, even though the contact was a bit hit and miss because she was unwell. I know my father didn't have much that was good to say about her, but I have to cling to some kind of hope.'

Until the mysteries of her past were cleared up, she was condemned to drift through an in-between world, where nothing was as it should be and her mind was flitting in all directions. 'I know things might not turn out well, but I have hazy memories of a loving and caring woman, and those are the recollections I want to cherish.'

He reached out and placed his hand on hers. His palm encompassed her small hand, and the warmth of his caring touch surged into her and gave her comfort.

'I hope it all turns out all right for you,' he said. She knew that he thought she was making a mistake, but he wasn't going to press his point home and she was thankful for that.

Their lunch was long and leisurely, as he had promised, and when they had eaten and drunk their fill, they started back across the bridge that spanned the lake.

'That was a lovely meal,' she said, 'but I've probably put on five pounds just looking at all that food.'

He gave her an amused glance. 'I doubt that. In the last few years your figure has hardly changed at all, except to become even more easy on the eye, if that was at all possible. You have a perfect figure.'

Did he really think that? A ripple of heat flushed her cheeks. She swallowed and said, 'Well, anyway, I'm the one who has to struggle into the jeans and skirts.'

They stood and looked over the lake, at the green expanse of the park beyond. Hannah said, 'Thank you for bringing me here, and for lunch. You were right. I needed the time out. I feel a lot calmer now.'

'I'm glad of that. I think you probably need to take more time for yourself whenever you can.'

'Perhaps.' She smiled at him. 'But I really ought to start thinking about going home. I have to pick up Ellie from her childminder.'

'I'll see you home,' he said. 'It'll be quicker and easier for you if I do that. I just need to stop off to pick up the car. It'll give me a chance to show you my apartment. You'll have time for that, won't you? I've just bought a new espresso machine and we can try it out.'

'An espresso machine…such decadence,' she said with a laugh. 'I'd love a cup of coffee, and I can't wait to see where you live. People have been telling me that it must be a fabulous place, and I just have to see it for myself.'

It didn't take them long to get there. A lift took them smoothly up to his Bayswater apartment, and they stepped out into an impressive hallway. Adam unlocked the door and ushered her inside. Hannah stood for a moment and looked around, awed by the beautiful surroundings. She hadn't known what to expect, but nothing on earth could have prepared her for this.

'It's…stunning,' she said, enthralled. She was standing in a long, rectangular reception room that was bordered along two sides with windows. They were draped with voile curtains that allowed in all the natural light, and the room was flooded with sunshine. From the angle of the sun, she guessed that the aspect was south facing.

The floor was wood finished, and the furnishings were luxurious…a couple of comfy, inviting settees, a glass-topped occasional table and an elegant white marble-fronted fireplace. There were plants set at intervals around the room, pale green frothy ferns and a beautiful arrangement of leaves and flowers on an elegant stand, to add colour to what was already perfection.

'Come and see the rest of the apartment,' he murmured. 'We're actually on the top floor, and that makes this place kind of special. It means I have the advantage of a roof terrace.'

He took her hand and led her over to the far side of the room and into a glass-walled conservatory. Looking out from that vantage point, Hannah's eyes widened as she took in the spectacular view of the city skyline. The room itself was set out as a breakfast room, with warm-coloured furnishings, a dining table and chairs. She could imagine him sitting here, reading his paper and glancing up every now and again to look out over the London cityscape.

From there, Adam showed her out onto an open roof terrace where there were seats set out to catch the warmth of the sun, along with another occasional table and tubs of flowers to add bright spots of colour. She gasped out aloud.

'This is all yours?' she said in a weak voice, looking at him with startled eyes.

'It's all mine,' he said. He tilted his head to one side, as though gauging her reaction. 'You like it, then?'

'Oh…that's an understatement,' she managed. 'It takes my breath away.' She walked over to the balcony rail, and looked out over Hyde Park and the city environs. 'Do you really mean to tell me that you actually bring yourself to leave this place and come into work every day?' Her eyes were wide with astonishment. 'How can you do that? I'd want to sit and drink it all in and not even think about moving from the spot.'

'Sit and enjoy,' he said with a smile, patting the

smooth surface of a bench seat that was shaded by a trellised screen. 'I'll go and make us some coffee.'

She did as he'd suggested, and leaned back against soft cushions, absorbing the light, sweet scent of flowers that filled the air.

He brought the coffee and set the cups down on the table, coming to sit beside her. They sipped the hot liquid and talked of nothing very much for a while, enjoying the tranquillity of the afternoon.

'You'd think it would be noisy, here in the city,' Hannah said quietly, 'but it's so peaceful, as though we're set apart from it. It's lovely out here.'

'It probably has to do with the way the balcony is screened. It cuts out the sound of the city, but still allows you to look out and enjoy the unspoiled view.'

Hannah nodded. She was silent for a while, her mind far away.

'You look thoughtful,' he said, a minute or so later. 'Is something wrong?'

'No, how could anything be wrong? I was just thinking how heavenly it is up here, and how easy it would be to simply forget your troubles and while away the hours.' Her gaze clouded momentarily. 'I wish Abby could see all this. She would think it was so cool.' She smiled, then said softly, 'And my mother...'

'You could bring her to visit...'

'Could I?' Hannah's mouth curved. 'She's very down-to-earth, my mum. I'm sure she'd say, "Wow, this is fantastic... I'd better not stop for long, though. Our Saxon will want to tear chunks out of that woodwork."'

Adam laughed. 'I can almost hear her saying that.'

He sobered, and said, 'There's something more, though, isn't there? Were you thinking of your natural mother?'

Hannah nodded. 'I wish I knew why it was so important to me that I find her. It colours everything I do, all my thoughts. It's as though I can't move on or settle to anything until that part of my life has been laid out for me so that I can see clearly what happened. I know she wasn't well and that she thought she couldn't care for me properly, but why did she just disappear from my life? I need to know the reasons.'

He reached for her, taking her into his arms and folding her to him. 'I know that's how you feel and I understand what's driving you, but it might be for the best if you never get to know the truth of it. How will you feel if your father was right about her?'

He ran a finger lightly down her cheek, tracing a line along the length of her jawbone to her chin. Then he gently tilted her face upwards and kissed her lightly on the mouth, the brush of his lips as soft as gossamer. 'Let me take away the worry and the hurt. I'll be here for you.'

Heat rippled through her veins. Her mouth trembled with unspoken need and he kissed her again, possessively this time, his lips making demands, seeking, coaxing, as though he would have her open up to him like a flower to the sun.

She felt the strength of his arms around her, keeping her close, drawing her to him, so that the fullness of her breasts was crushed against the hard wall of his chest. A warm tide of desire ran through her.

'I want you, Hannah,' he said, his voice rough around the edges. 'I could make you forget, if only you would let me.' His hand stroked along the length of her, along the curve of her hip, lingering on the smooth, silky expanse of her thigh.

'Would you?' she whispered. 'I wish… I wish I could be sure, but…' She gazed up at him and asked the question that haunted her. 'Do you think you would ever want to give up your London life and go back to the countryside?' Would he ever want to be with her, stay with her?

'That wasn't in my grand plan,' he murmured. 'Does it matter that much?' He looked into her eyes and smiled, and bent to kiss her once again, his lips leaving a trail of fire along the creamy line of her shoulder and making a detour over the swell of her breast. Her whole body shook in response, a slow tingle of expectation that started up in her abdomen and spread outwards.

She wanted him, too. It seemed as though she had yearned for him for a lifetime, but an inner caution held her back. How could there ever be any future for her with him? He didn't love her. In all this time, he had never told her that love was on his mind, and why would he?

They had nothing in common. Their lives were so far apart…you only had to look at this magnificent apartment and compare it with her tiny flat to see that. She couldn't see herself living and working in the city for the rest of her days…and hadn't he just made it clear that he would never think of leaving this place?

She put up a trembling hand and held him back. 'Perhaps we both had a little too much wine with our meal,' she said, with a small frown. 'I think it must have gone to my head.'

'I didn't have any,' he said, shaking his head. 'I'm on call, so I have to stay away from alcohol.'

She blinked. 'I didn't drink the whole bottle,' she mumbled, trying to clear her thoughts. 'Did I?'

'No, you didn't.' His mouth indented. 'Don't worry about it.'

She straightened up and avoided his gaze. 'I should go,' she said. 'I have to go and fetch Ellie.'

He nodded, and just then his pager bleeped. Pulling a face, he checked it and reached for his mobile. 'I'll call you a taxi,' he said. 'I have to go back in to work. There's been a multiple RTA and they need extra support.'

'I'll catch the tube,' she said, but he cut off her words.

'No, you won't. I'll pay for the taxi and the driver will take you wherever you need to go. You could get him to take you to pick up Ellie and then ask him to drive you home…whatever you need to do.'

He stood up in one fluid movement and made ready to leave.

It took Hannah a little longer to compose herself, but she walked with him to the lift, and he saw her into the cab just a short time later. He was already distancing himself from her. His mind was on his work, she could see that, and it only went to underline her basic instinct. He didn't love her. Mentally, he was already moving on.

CHAPTER EIGHT

'I WANT to see my mummy,' Ellie said. 'Why can't I go and see her? I made her a picture and I want to take it to her.'

'I know you do, sweetheart,' Hannah murmured. She finished washing the last of the crockery and left the pots to drain. Hurriedly, she wiped her hands on a teatowel, and went over to the little girl. 'Just as soon as the doctor says it's all right, I'll take you to see her, I promise.' She put an arm around Ellie's shoulders. 'I know it's hard for you, not being able to see your mummy as you used to, but we saw her yesterday, didn't we? You gave her a big kiss.'

Ellie's lip was jutting. 'Want to see her today.'

'She wasn't feeling very well today. Anyway, I thought we could go and buy her some flowers in the morning, so that she'll have a nice surprise when we go and see her tomorrow. Which flower does she like best, do you know?'

'Roses. Ones that smell nice. She loves those.'

'Good. Those are what we'll get for her, then.' Hannah went to a cupboard and brought out some tissue paper left over from a present-wrapping session. 'Shall I show you how to make some flowers out of tissue paper? I bet we can make some really pretty ones.'

Ellie nodded, intrigued, and came to sit down at the table, watching as Hannah cut the coloured paper and twisted it into shape. 'See, doesn't that look lovely? Now we need to fix it with some wire, to make a stem. I'll have to see if I can find some.'

Ellie was momentarily distracted and started to make flowers of her own accord. Watching her, Hannah breathed a small sigh of relief. It was difficult sometimes, not knowing what to do to soothe the child and keep her happy.

Abby's condition had improved a little, after a brief setback, but the medical team wanted her to get as much rest as possible. Hannah had gone to visit her every day, and she had taken Ellie with her as often as was possible, but obviously it wasn't often enough as far as Ellie was concerned.

'We'll go and see her early tomorrow morning, if you like, before I start work.' It would mean dropping Ellie off at her childminder's house afterwards, instead of taking her straight to nursery school, but that was a small price to pay.

The flower shop was closed when they set off after breakfast next day, but Ellie didn't seem to be too upset about that. She was clutching the paper flowers they had made, and she was waiting expectantly to see how her mother would react to them.

Hannah felt good inside. Two letters had arrived in the post that morning, and they were both from the same source, the missing persons line, and one of them was for Abby. She wondered how her friend would respond to her own surprise package.

'Oh, they are so beautiful,' Abby said, her face lighting up in a smile when she saw the flowers. 'Thank you, Ellie. These are lovely.'

'We was going to get you real ones, but the shop was closed.'

'These are just as pretty. They're perfect.'

It was good to see that Abby was looking better today, and after a while Hannah gently broached the subject that was on her mind. 'I had a letter this morning,' she said, 'from the missing persons agency. They've given me a phone number to pass on to you… It's your parents' number, I believe, and there's an address, but neither of them are the same as the ones you had. Do you think you might feel up to giving them a call later on?'

Abby's mouth dropped open, and her eyes widened. 'How did the agency manage to find them?'

'I'm not sure. They checked the electoral register for different areas, as far as I know. It took a while, and I suppose there's a chance that they may have the wrong people, but at least the agency managed to come through with a result.' Hannah handed the letter to Abby.

'I don't know what to say.' Abby sank back against her pillows. 'Thank you for doing all this for me, Hannah. I'll have to think about it for a bit and try to take everything on board. For some reason it's taking a while to sink in.'

'Don't hassle yourself. It was bound to have come as a bit of a shock. Just try to rest and concentrate on getting well again. Ellie wants you home.'

Ellie sat on the bed and snuggled in the crook of her mother's arm. 'You come home soon?' she asked.

'Just as soon as I can,' Abby promised.

When Hannah walked into A and E half an hour later, Adam was assigning patients for treatment. 'You can take the angina patient,' he told her. 'Sarah has put him on an ECG, but he's not responding to glyceryl trinitrate.'

'I'll go and take a look at him.'

Adam stopped her as she would have walked away. His hand lightly gripped her arm and he was looking at her oddly. 'You seem different this morning…though I'm not sure what it is that's changed. Has something happened? Is your friend, Abby, being discharged from hospital?'

She shook her head. 'Not yet. I'm hopeful that it won't be too long before that happens, though, and in the meantime we've had news of her parents. Or, at least, we think we've found them.'

'I'm glad for her…but there's something else, isn't there?' His eyes narrowed. 'Does it have something to do with your search for your mother? Has something turned up?'

She nodded. 'I'm trying not to get too excited about it just yet. These things have a way of not turning out as you expect, but the missing persons line has given me the name of a company where my mother used to work at one time. Apparently she was a textile designer there. There's a possibility that they might have a forwarding address, or they might be able to tell me some-thing about her. Anyway, I'm going to follow it up just as soon as I have the time…perhaps later, after I finish work.'

She had already made up her mind to give Ryan a call and see if it was possible for him to come and sit with Ellie while she went to find the place.

'Perhaps you had better leave early. These organisa-tions tend to keep to business hours. If we're not too busy then, I'll arrange cover for you.'

'Would you?' She gave him a beaming smile. 'Thanks, Adam. It means so much to me.' She laid a hand lightly on his arm but he shifted away from her and her hand slid down.

'I know it does.' He didn't say any more, but turned away to attend to his patients, leaving her stung by that sudden rejection. Why had he done that? Was he re-membering how she had ultimately pushed him away that day at his apartment, or did he still believe that no good would come of her search?

She couldn't talk to him about any of that now, though. He wasn't in a receptive mood, and she doubted she would get anywhere for her trouble. Right now her work had to take priority.

She went in search of her patient. He was in a good deal of pain, and was clearly anxious about what was happening to him. She carefully examined him.

'I'm going to give you an injection to relieve the dis-comfort,' she told him, after a while, 'and I'm going to set up an infusion of glyceryl trinitrate, so that you should soon be feeling much better. It should work better for you that way, rather than taking it by mouth as you've been used to doing.'

Adam came and found her a few minutes later. 'How's it going? Is his condition improving at all?'

'Not really,' she said. 'I'm worried that the angina is unstable and I think he probably needs to go for angiography.'

He nodded. 'Contact Cardiology and have someone come down and take a look at him. With any luck, they'll probably want to come and deal with it right away.'

'I'll do that.'

She went back to her patient and carefully explained to him what might happen.

'Why do I need to see a surgeon?' he asked. 'I've always just had tablets before.'

'The tablets don't seem to be very effective any more,' she told him. 'We think that there could be an obstruction in your artery that is hampering your circulation and causing you pain. The surgeon will try to remove that obstruction.'

'Are they going to cut me open?'

Hannah shook her head. 'Nothing as drastic as that. You'll be given a local anaesthetic so that you won't feel any pain from the procedure, and then the surgeon will insert a catheter into the artery at your groin and feed it upwards until it meets the obstruction. He'll try to remove whatever's causing the problem.'

He seemed resigned to the procedure and, having gained his consent some time later, Hannah left him in the care of the cardiologist.

She was so busy for the rest of the day that she hardly had time to think about the letter sitting in her pocket. She wanted to follow up the lead about her mother more than anything, but work had to come first and she had to make a determined effort to concentrate on the job in hand.

Her angina patient was scheduled for angiography early that afternoon, and Hannah had to ensure that he was comfortable in the meantime. She was glad when the surgeon finally came and told her that the procedure had gone well.

'You should go now,' Adam told her, when she had finished writing up her notes. 'I'll take over for you from here.' He sent her a quick look. 'Are you going straight to the company's address, or do you have to go home first?'

'I'll go and collect Ellie and see her settled at home. I've asked Ryan to come over and stay with her, but he has to go for a meeting with his tutor and might not be able to get away on time.' She glanced at her watch. 'It's early yet, though. I might give the company's personnel officer a call and let her know when I expect to arrive there. I spoke to her earlier, and she said they're not really supposed to tell me anything, and she couldn't guarantee any information, but in the circumstances she would do her best to see if they have something on file. I'm just hoping that she'll be able to give me some clue as to what might have happened to my mother.'

'Good luck.'

She gave him a lopsided smile. 'Thanks.' It was

strange talking to him this way. He was so close to her that she could have touched him if she were just to reach out a hand, but after the way he had reacted to her that morning, she was wary of doing that. It was as though an invisible wall separated them and neither one of them was prepared to breach it.

She went back to the flat and waited for Ryan to arrive. Ellie was in a fractious mood, and it took all Hannah's ingenuity to find ways to pacify her.

'I don't like my nursery school,' Ellie stormed. 'It's horrible. They made me drink milk and I hate milk.'

Hannah sent her a thoughtful look. 'You drink milk when I give it to you.' She didn't know what to make of this latest rebellion.

'Your milk's different.' Ellie glared at Hannah. 'I'm not going to school again.'

'Oh, dear. That's a shame. I thought you liked seeing your friends at school. You'll miss them if you don't go.'

'Don't care. I want my mummy.'

Hannah winced, at a loss for the moment, but just then the doorbell rang, and she hurried to let Ryan into the flat.

'You made it, then,' she said with a smile. 'Thanks for coming over. I was a bit undecided whether to ring you… I wasn't sure whether all your exams were over and done with.'

'They're all over now, so it's no problem. We're all just biding our time, from here on, waiting on the results.'

'How do you think you've done? Is it hard to say, or do you think they went all right?'

He made a face. 'All right, I think. My tutor seems to feel that I don't need to worry about my grades, anyway.'

'Does he?' Hannah smiled. 'That's brilliant. I'm glad for you.' She paused. 'I take it that you've made up for arguing with him, then?'

Ryan nodded. 'He's been loosing his cool lately, but he's not a bad sort, when all's said and done. I think he was worried about cuts in staffing at the college, but he's been told his job's safe, so he's calmed right down.'

'I'm glad.' Hannah put her arms around him and gave him a hug. 'I knew it wasn't your fault that you argued.'

A discreet cough made her turn around, and she stared in surprise to see that Adam was standing in the room.

'Adam…you startled me.' She frowned. 'What are you doing here? How did you get in?'

'The door was open,' he said. 'In fact, both this door and the front door downstairs were open. I did knock, but you obviously didn't hear me.' He sent Ryan a grim look. 'Perhaps you were too busy.'

What had he meant by that? She let her arms drop to her sides and she straightened her shoulders.

She was still unsure about exactly what was going on, or what had brought him here. 'I was just getting ready to go,' she said. 'Ryan's going to stay with Ellie for me.'

Adam nodded. 'I came as soon as my shift ended. I thought that if he didn't manage to get here, I could help out myself, but I can see that's not necessary after all.' He glanced around, still unsmiling. 'Where is Ellie? She isn't usually this quiet, is she?'

Hannah's gaze darted around the room. 'I expect she's in the bathroom,' she said. She went to check, but there was no sign of the little girl, and she glanced into the kitchen in case she had gone in there. 'I don't understand. She was here just a minute ago.' She was frowning now, a sudden feeling of panic growing inside her.

She looked back at the door and saw that there was a small imprint in the velvet-upholstered lid of the toy box that was placed to one side of it. Her pulse quickened. 'Do you think she climbed up and opened the door? She's growing fast, and perhaps she can reach the doorhandle.'

Panicking now, she flung open the door and raced downstairs. There was still no sign of Ellie. The hallway was empty and the front door was closed, but she guessed that Adam must have done that when he'd come in. When Hannah looked about her, she could see that Ellie might have been able to reach up and open it, perhaps by climbing up onto the low umbrella stand that was to one side. It was long and rectangular, and sturdy enough to hold her weight.

By now, Ryan and Adam had come downstairs to join her. 'Have you checked all around?' she asked. 'I can't find her.'

'She's nowhere in this building,' Adam said. 'I've tried Dean's flat and Abby's, but they're both locked up and there's no sound of anyone in there.'

Ryan looked concerned. 'She can't have gone far, can she? She was here when I arrived just a little while ago.'

Hannah pulled open the front door and looked down

the street. There were no children to be seen. 'Where can she have gone?' Her mind was racing, but her anxious thoughts were getting her nowhere. 'I know she's upset about school, and she's missing her mother, but surely she wouldn't just have run out blindly, not caring where she was going?'

'I'll go and look down the street,' Ryan said. He set off at a sprint, looking around him as he went, and Hannah went to follow him outside.

'Stop for a minute and think,' Adam said, laying a hand on her arm and holding her back. 'What might she have had in mind? Does she know where you go to get to the underground station? Would she be likely to try to get to the hospital?'

Hannah shook her head. 'I wouldn't have thought she'd remember the way.' Her brow indented. 'We went to see Abby this morning, and I wouldn't have expected her to be so desperate as to go there on her own. She would be too frightened.'

'Where else might she go? Is there anything she wanted apart from her mother? Anything she was upset about?'

'I can't think straight. My mind's all over the place.'

'Take your time.'

Ryan came back, his breath coming in short bursts. 'I've been down the street both ways and checked the road junctions. I can't see her anywhere.' He paused to suck air into his lungs. 'I'll try the neighbours.'

'She wanted to give Abby some flowers,' Hannah said, looking up at Adam, 'but we were too early this morning and the shop was closed. I can't see that she would have gone there now, though. She knows that you need money to buy them, and she doesn't have any.'

Adam was thoughtful. 'What about a garden nearby?' He glanced around. 'Are there any gardens around here, where she might have gone?'

'Yes…' A spark of hope sprang into life inside her. 'There's a park, just a couple of streets away from here—it's only small, but there are lawns and a shrubbery and a formal rose garden. It's possible that she could have gone there.'

Ryan came back from exploring the houses on either side. 'I can't find her,' he said. 'Shall I wait here while you go and look for her, in case she comes back?'

'Would you?' Hannah laid a hand fleetingly on his arm. 'Thanks, Ryan. There's a faint chance that she might have gone to look at the roses. Perhaps she had it in her head to pick some for her mother.'

She hurried away, and Adam went with her. By the time they arrived at the park, she was out of breath from rushing, and they decided to split up and go in opposite directions to cover both sides of the gardens.

Hannah skirted the stone-built water fountain and ran across the grass. Slowing down, she turned onto the footpath and approached the rose beds. Her heart was pounding so fast that she could feel the pulse thumping in her throat. Then she stopped and stood still. There, over on the far side of the beautifully laid out patchwork of flowers, a small child was reaching out to touch a pink rose.

Hannah walked up to her, going to stand quietly next to the little girl.

'Mummy likes these,' Ellie told her. 'I want to give Mummy some flowers like these ones.' She glanced up at Hannah. 'Can I pick one?'

Hannah shook her head. 'I'm sorry, but the park-keeper won't let us do that.'

'Why?'

'We're not allowed to take the flowers, because if we do that there will be none left for other people to enjoy.'

'Why?'

Hannah's mouth made an odd little quirk, but she was still too taken aback by what had happened for her to be able to answer the impossible question. Instead, she laid a hand on Ellie's shoulder. 'We'll go and see if we can buy some from the flower shop. It should still be open.'

She was too overwhelmed at finding Ellie to be cross with her for giving her such a fright. Later, when she was calmer, she would give her the lecture about not running away. For now, she was content to hug the child and satisfy herself that she was safe.

Adam came and stood beside her. 'Well, that's a relief,' he said.

Hannah nodded. 'Let's get her home, shall we?' She gave a faint smile. 'I need to stop by the florist on the way.'

Adam's mouth made a wry shape. 'I guessed as much.'

Ryan was glad to see them arrive. 'Thank heaven for that,' he said. He looked at Ellie. 'We thought we'd lost you,' he said. 'We were all very worried.'

'Why?' Ellie asked.

'Because we didn't know where you were.'

'Why?'

Adam made a coughing sound, covering a laugh, and Hannah did her best to hide a smile.

'You went out without telling us where you were going,' she said. 'I thought you were in the sitting room, but when I looked around, you had gone. I was very worried. I didn't know where to look for you.'

Ellie gave her a quizzical look, and she might have said something, but Ryan cut in, 'I'll take you to see your mummy, if you like.'

'Now?'

'Yes, right now. Let's hurry up and get ready to go.' He glanced at Hannah. 'You should go and call on the personnel officer. I doubt she'll wait around for much longer.'

Hannah gave a start. 'Yes…I'd almost forgotten. Will you be able to wait around here for me after you've been to the hospital? Are you staying the night, or do you have to get back?'

'I can stay the night,' Ryan told her, 'so you don't need to worry about rushing home.'

'Thanks.' She glanced at Adam. 'It was really thoughtful of you to come over to help out. I didn't expect you to do that.'

'I know how much it means to you to find your mother.' His expression was serious, and now he glanced down at his watch. 'Time's running on. I'll give you a lift over to the company's office.'

'Thanks.'

They set off a little while later. Adam didn't say

much on the drive over there, and Hannah wondered what was occupying his thoughts. She said, 'I don't think I would have known where to begin looking for Ellie if you hadn't made me stop and get myself together. I needed that breathing space.'

'It's hard to think logically when you're upset. I imagine Ellie was working on the same principle. Her mother was uppermost in her mind, and she wanted to please her.' He manoeuvred the car through the traffic and then added, 'Ryan must have know that when he decided to take her to see Abby. She won't settle until she's given her the flowers.'

'You're probably right.' She sent him an oblique glance. 'I thought Ryan was really good, the way he went looking for her. He just shot off and did whatever he could to make sure that she wasn't nearby.'

Adam's expression didn't change. 'Yes, he was quick thinking and he did the right thing.'

It didn't sound as though his impression of Ryan had changed, though. His attitude was much the same as it had been before…as though there was still a line dividing them. Hannah was disappointed.

'Ryan has been trying really hard lately to make things work,' she said cautiously. 'He's cleared up his debts, and he's been working really hard on his studies. He says the exams went well. He even patched up the dispute with his tutor, though it wasn't his fault that they argued to begin with.'

'He's lucky that he's had you to champion him,' Adam murmured. 'You always had faith in him and took the time to help him make the best of himself.' He looked at her searchingly. 'You care very deeply for him, don't you? There's a very strong bond between the two of you.'

She nodded. 'We've been through a lot together.'

He didn't say any more, but announced a moment or two later, 'We're here. This must be the place. I'll wait here for you.'

'Are you sure?'

He nodded. Perhaps he didn't want to intrude on her personal space, but Hannah was nervous at the prospect of talking to someone who had news about her mother. Deep inside, she would have welcomed his support, or been thankful for his comforting presence. He had come this far, though, and she wasn't going to push the issue.

The personnel officer was friendly and generally understanding of the situation, but she said, 'I'm not supposed to give information out. All I'm actually allowed to do is to confirm that this person worked here at one time.' Her expression was sympathetic. 'I'm sorry... I wish I could tell you more.'

Hannah was crestfallen. 'I'm desperate for news of my mother,' she said. 'I was fostered, and then adopted, and now I've come to London to look for her. I've been trying to trace her for the last few months, but I haven't had any success, and this is the only hope I have of finding her. Did you know her at all? Could you tell me that? Any small thing would be a help.'

The woman shook her head. 'I've only worked here for around five years, and I didn't know your mother at all.' She hesitated, and then seemed to relent. She said quietly, confidentially, 'She worked for the company some twelve years ago, as a freelance textile designer, but she was only here for a short time. We still use some of her designs, though. I could show you, if you like?'

'Could you?' Hannah's heart gave a sudden lurch. 'Thank you… Yes, I'd like that, very much.'

Hannah was intrigued by the work that the woman showed her. The fabric samples were beautiful, with delicate patterns embroidered into the material or with thread woven into an embossed feature.

'Your mother is a very talented woman.'

Hannah nodded. 'Yes, I can see that she is.' She hesitated. 'Do you know why she left, or where she might have gone from here? I don't suppose you had a forwarding address.'

The woman flicked through the file drawer. 'I'm afraid I have very little. As far as I can gather, her mother died some six months before she left us. That would be your grandmother, wouldn't it? There's a resignation note in her file that tells us she wanted to move on after she had finished dealing with her mother's estate. Other than that, there's not much more I can tell you, I'm afraid.'

'Could I have the letter, do you think? Or maybe a copy of it?' It wasn't much, but it looked as though that was all she might ever have of her mother.

'I'll make a photocopy for the file, and you can have the original, if you like…just don't tell anyone that I was the one who gave it to you.' The woman gave her a sympathetic smile. 'I'm sorry that I'm not able to help you any more than that. As it is, we usually throw out any records after a certain length of time, so you've been fortunate that we still have these on file. Everything else has been updated onto the computers, and there's no information about your mother on there.'

'Thank you for your help, anyway,' Hannah murmured. She glanced down at the letter, brushing a finger lightly over the handwritten words as though that would bring her closer to the woman she hadn't seen for so long.

She went outside to where Adam was waiting for her in the car.

'Was it any help?' Adam asked as he opened the car door for her and watched her slide into the passenger seat.

'Not really,' Hannah said. 'There was just this letter of resignation. The address is my grandmother's house, and I've already looked at that and come to a stop.' She pressed her lips together to stop them from trembling. 'At least I have something that was hers.' She showed the letter to Adam, and then when he handed it back to her, she folded it carefully and pushed it into the pocket of her jacket. Her hands were shaking, and she clasped her fingers together to hold them still.

'I'm sorry,' he said. 'I know that you were hoping for a lot more.' He drew her to him, wrapping his arms around her, and that simple act was her undoing. Salt tears trickled down her cheeks, and she buried her face into his shoulder, quietly weeping for what might have been.

His hand gently stroked the silk of her hair, and she let him soothe her, absorbing the comfort of his nearness, his undemanding gentleness.

Slowly she cried herself out, and then gradually

began to pull herself together. She brushed the dampness from her cheeks with trembling fingers and tried to make herself presentable again.

'I'm all right,' she said, straightening. 'I'm sorry. I should have tried to hold it all together.'

'Crying is probably the best thing you can do. It will do you good to let it all out and to let go. It's one of the ways that we start to heal.'

'Perhaps.'

'Is there anything that I can do?' He ran a finger lightly along her cheek, as though satisfying himself that she really was over the worst. Then he moved back from her and simply looked at her, waiting for her response.

'I think I've come to the end of the line,' she said huskily. 'I don't see any other avenue to explore.'

She was quiet for a moment, and then said, 'Perhaps I'll never know the truth of what happened, but I do believe that my mother didn't do anything wrong, no matter what my father might have implied. How could he be the judge of her? Perhaps he let his guilty conscience do the talking. Throughout my childhood, he hardly ever made much of an attempt to take care of me, but I never heard my mother say a bad word about him.'

'What will you do now? Do you have any idea?'

'I think I'll go home to the Chilterns and try to get on with my life when my stint in A and E here finishes. I've always been relatively secure there, and I know my mum will be pleased to have me nearby. She worries about how I'm doing.'

'So you're giving up? You're planning to run away?'

She stiffened. 'If you want to put it like that, yes.'

He turned on the car's ignition and began the drive home. He didn't say very much, and Hannah was lost in her own thoughts.

Had he wondered whether she might want to stay on in London? He hadn't asked her to do that, and she honestly didn't know whether she was up to it.

Being close to him had taught her one thing above all…she wanted him to stay close by. She wanted to see him and be with him, and most of all she wanted him to feel the same way about her. She loved him, that had become clearer to her day by day, week by week, but it had come as no surprise. She had always known that he was special.

The trouble was that in following through on that love, wouldn't she be copying the pattern set by her mother, in loving a man who was more interested in his career prospects than he was in wanting to be with her?

CHAPTER NINE

''BYE, sweetheart. I'll see you later,' Hannah said, waving to Ellie as the childminder led her into the house.

Ellie blew her a kiss. 'Bye, Hannah.' She clutched her teddy bear tightly to her chest, but she was smiling, and Hannah began to relax a little.

'She seems a lot happier this morning,' Ryan commented as they headed towards the hospital. 'I think seeing her mother last night must have helped.'

Hannah nodded. 'I'm sure it did. She was much chattier when she came home, and I managed to have a talk with her about what has been upsetting her, lately—apart from her mother being in hospital, of course.'

'Did you find out what the problem was?'

'I think so. It's all to do with her teddy bear, apparently. She likes to keep him with her all the time, but the teachers have been asking her to leave him in a bag in the cloakroom during the day, in case one of the other children takes a fancy to him. They're afraid of personal items going astray.'

Ryan lifted a brow. 'Poor little thing. I can see how she wouldn't like that.'

'I've had a word with the childminder about it, so that she'll be able to talk to the teachers and explain the situation, and I've written Ellie's name on a ribbon and sewn it around the bear's neck, so hopefully they'll have no objections to her keeping him with her.'

They arrived at the hospital, and Hannah started towards A and E. 'Will you be going back to college later on?' she asked, glancing back at Ryan.

'That's what I planned to do. I'm going up to the ward to see Abby for a while first, but I'll come down to A and E and say goodbye before I go.'

'OK. I'll talk to you later, then.'

Hannah pushed open the door of the emergency department and went to prepare for her first patient of the day. She saw that Mr Tremayne was on duty today, and her spirits drooped as she realised that Adam was probably not going to be around.

'He's gone to a meeting with management about the new consultant post,' Sarah told her, as they began to treat a woman whose heart rate was too rapid and causing her to collapse.

Hannah grimaced inwardly. It shouldn't have come as any surprise to her that he was still in talks about the job. Adam was ambitious, and he'd made no secret of the fact that he wanted this opportunity…but even so, she had clung to the hope that he might reconsider.

If he wasn't so determined to stay on in London, there might have been a faint chance that she would meet up with him again, some time in the future, closer to home. She couldn't bear the thought of not being near him, and at the same time she desperately wanted to be near her own home and family.

'I suppose they must be getting ready to announce the appointment,' she said. She worked carefully as she spoke, inserting an intravenous cannula and giving the woman an initial dose of adenosine.

'I imagine it's a foregone conclusion,' Sarah murmured. 'Adam really wants a consultant post, and he's always said that this hospital is second to none.'

Hannah tried not to think about that. 'You might feel a slight sensation of flushing and a little chest discomfort to begin with,' she told her patient, 'but it's nothing to worry about. This should help to bring your heart rate down.'

Sarah recorded a rhythm strip and Hannah studied it briefly. 'That seems to be doing the trick,' she told the woman with a brief smile a short time later. 'We'll see how you go for a while, and then I'll refer you to Cardiology. They'll take over your care from here.'

She went over to the desk to put a call through to Cardiology. Sarah followed, filing the ECG strip along with the patient's notes.

'Have you made up your mind what you'll do when your appointment here comes to an end?' she asked. 'Have you sorted out another job yet?'

'I'm going to apply for a posting nearer home,' Hannah said. 'I keep longing for the valleys and the streams and the woods. It's peaceful near where my mum lives in the Chilterns, and I think I'll try to get work with a general practitioner over there. I heard that there should be a place for me at a surgery close to home.'

'We'll miss you,' Sarah said.

'Me, too. I'll be sorry to leave everyone behind.' Especially Adam, but it was best not to think about that. It hurt too much.

She moved away from the desk and went to find her next patient. For the rest of the morning, she tried to immerse herself in her work. That way, she had less time to think of her own problems and it helped to numb her own inner pain in some small way.

Adam came into the department just as she was about to go for a coffee break, and she tried to read his expression in an attempt to discover whether he was pleased with the outcome of his meeting. She didn't want to ask him how things had gone. She wasn't ready to hear outright that he had been given the job. Where would that leave her, other than nursing her loss back home?

He was giving nothing away, though. Instead, he murmured, 'Did I see Ryan come in with you this morning?'

She nodded. 'That's right. He's going back to college later, and then he said he planned to go home and spend some time with our mum and dad.'

'Oh? Has he said anything to you about his search for a job, now that he's close to finishing his course? Is he likely to be looking for something back home?'

'He hasn't said too much about it, but I know he's looking around. It seems that we're in the same boat, with my job coming to an end and his college course finishing.'

He gave her a quick, assessing glance. 'Are you still thinking of going home, too?'

'That's what I had in mind, yes.'

'Have you given up on finding your natural mother here in London? You were upset yesterday, but I wondered if you might feel differently about things in the light of day.'

'I don't know what else to try. I've pursued every avenue I can think of and all of the agencies have drawn a blank.'

'Yes, I know it hasn't been easy. The trail just seemed to vanish, didn't it? It occurred to me, though, that your mother was working in the area some twelve years ago, and there could be a good reason why she dropped out of sight after that.'

'Apart from deliberately concealing her where-abouts, you mean?'

He nodded. 'She was ill when you were very young, and then she had a nervous breakdown and suffered from bouts of illness, which I'm assuming was why you were eventually adopted. It could be that the illness con-tinued, and perhaps she was in hospital for some of the time. Has anyone checked hospital records?'

'I believe so, but nothing surfaced. Anyway, she was well enough to work for a while, and to take time out to sell my grandmother's house and consider freelan-cing.'

'That's the point, though, isn't it? Perhaps she wasn't able to go on doing freelance work. Isn't it possible that she was taken ill again?'

'I suppose so… Or she might have been an addict

or an alcoholic…that's what my father seemed to suggest.'

'He probably said that because he didn't understand what was wrong with her, and he didn't take the trouble to find out.' He looked at her searchingly.

'There is one way that we might be able to find out more…through hospital admissions records. These things are highly confidential, of course, and it all depends on whether I'll be able to obtain the relevant permissions to pass on certain information. I could try to do that, if you like. Would you let me do that for you?'

She was startled by his offer. 'I thought you said it would be best left alone? You said I might not like what I found.'

'Perhaps I was wrong.' He grimaced. 'If we could clear up the mystery of what happened to her, it might help you to be able to move on. What do you say?'

'All right.' She gave him a faltering smile. 'You're really my last hope.'

He gave her hand a light squeeze. 'Leave it with me. I'll do my best to find her for you.'

'Thank you.' Hannah wasn't sure what to think. He was helping her, and he was being kind and considerate, and more than anything she wanted to reach up to him and put her arms around him and thank him for trying. Something held her back, though, and perhaps it was the thought that he might just do this one thing for her and then he would prepare to move on once again.

He became briskly efficient, assessing the list of

patients waiting to be seen and prioritising them. 'I'll be in treatment room two, if I'm needed,' he said. He glanced at Sarah, who had come to look through the charts. 'Will you come and assist? I need to reduce a fracture.'

'Of course.'

Hannah went back to work, trying to concentrate her attention on her patients, but she saw Ryan walk into A and E just a short time later, looking pleased with himself.

'Has something happened?' Hannah asked. She put the collection of lab reports that she had been scanning to one side. 'You're looking very bright and breezy. Have you had some good news?'

He nodded, coming over to her. 'I've just heard that they're sending Abby home today. She's looking so much better than she was just a few days ago.'

'I'm glad,' Hannah said with a smile. 'Ellie will be so pleased.'

He nodded, but hesitated as Adam came to join them at the desk. Adam glanced at Ryan and inclined his head in a greeting, but said nothing.

'Yes, I think she will be,' Ryan went on. 'Of course, she's going to have to adjust to the fact that she has grandparents… I've just been introduced to Abby's mother and father, up on the ward.'

'Really?' Hannah was startled. 'I didn't think they would get together so soon. Did everything work out all right for them? Did the meeting go all right? It's been so long since they last saw Abby.'

'Yes, to all of that.' Ryan laughed. 'It sounds as though there was a mix-up over communication. They moved house and Abby's letters to them weren't forwarded on to the new place, and then Abby moved to a bigger flat and changed her phone number and everything became confused. They seem to have sorted out everything now, though.'

'I'm so relieved.' Hannah was happy for her friend. 'I'll have to see if I can be home in time to welcome her back. Are her parents going to take her home?'

'Yes, they've just been making the arrangements.'

'That's wonderful news.' She turned to Adam. 'It is, isn't it? We've all been so worried about her.'

Adam nodded. He glanced at Ryan and said, 'You've been a good friend to Abby, and to Ellie, these last few weeks. I suppose you must have taken on board that she was in a difficult position, as a single mother, with no contact with her parents. It must have been fairly easy for you and Hannah to identify with her, given your own family backgrounds.'

'That's true enough. I suppose you could say that, in a way, there's a kind of unspoken bond between us.' He sent Adam a curious glance. 'I wouldn't really have expected you to notice what I was doing, or to take all that on board. I've always been the black sheep where you and your family were concerned.'

'I don't think I would agree with that. It has been obvious that you've had a lot to contend with yourself lately, what with exams and the problems with your accommodation and so on. Things must have been difficult for you, but you still took the time to help out with Ellie.' He paused, looking thoughtful for a moment or two. 'I think Hannah has been glad of that, and she tells me that in spite of everything you might have done all right with your studies.'

Hannah sent him a quick, puzzled look. She hadn't known him to talk like this to Ryan in a long time. Perhaps things were different now because Ryan was showing that he was more receptive to what he had to say.

'I don't have the results yet,' Ryan murmured, 'but, yes, I think it might work out all right. My tutor glanced through the papers and says I shouldn't worry.'

'That sounds encouraging. What about the problem with your accommodation? I couldn't help hearing that you were having difficulties over various debts. I know it can be difficult for students to keep on top of things.'

Ryan didn't immediately jump to his own defence as he might have done at one time. Perhaps it showed the measure of his good humour now that Abby was finally coming home.

'Eventually, I did, with Hannah's help. The thing is, I used to share the accommodation with some other students, and they dropped out one by one, and went off without paying what they owed. The debts were all theirs, but I was left to carry the can. I've managed to persuade a couple of them to cough up, though.' He sent Hannah a quick look. 'I've put the money to one side, so that I can pay you back what I owe.'

'I told you, you don't need to worry about that,' she said. 'I'm sure you have lots of other things on your mind right now. Not least the worry of finding a job now that your course has come to an end.'

Ryan grimaced. 'That's true enough.'

Adam studied him. 'Have you thought about where you might apply for work?'

Ryan nodded. 'I've put out some feelers, and I've a few interviews lined up, but my final decision will depend on what Abby wants to do, really. I need to talk to her about it some more, but I'll settle for something that will suit both of us. If she wants to move back near to where her parents are living, then I'll look for something close to there.'

Adam looked as though that surprised him. 'Are you saying that you and Abby are a couple?' He watched him, his head tilted slightly to one side, as though he wasn't sure what to make of him.

Ryan nodded, smiling. 'I've liked Abby from the time I first met her. She and I just seemed to click somehow. Anyway, we're not going to rush into anything, because I have to find work first of all, but as soon as I have my career sorted out, we'll make it official.'

Hannah hugged him. 'Ryan, you didn't say a word. How long were you planning on keeping it to yourself? I'm so pleased for you.' She smiled up at him. 'Of course, I did sort of guess, when you kept finding a reason to go off and visit her.'

Adam was staring at both of them, looking perplexed. 'I had no idea what was going on,' he said. He looked preoccupied all at once. 'You know,' he added, turning his attention to Ryan, 'if you have any trouble finding work, and you decide to move back to near where your foster-mother lives, I'm sure my father would be able to find you some work on the estate.'

Ryan's brow furrowed. 'I would have to think about

that. I'm not at all sure that it would be an option. Your father kicked me out, remember? I was accused of stealing, and no one believed anything I had to say. As I recall, he was never too happy about having me around.'

Adam frowned. 'I don't believe he ever actually outright accused you of stealing and, in fact, the reason he let you go was because you were volatile and too quick to anger. It caused too much of a problem with the other workers, and you weren't able to change the way you behaved.'

He studied Ryan for a moment. 'Over the years, my father has shown enough interest in your progress to talk to your foster-mother about how you've been doing, and I think he realises that you were young and unsure of yourself back then. I'm sure he appreciates the problems you had to overcome, and he must know that you've calmed down over the years.'

Hannah looked at Adam, wide-eyed. 'I didn't know that he had kept in touch with our mother. You didn't say anything.'

'I doubt you would have believed me.' He glanced back at Ryan. 'Anyway, bear it in mind. I'm sure there won't be a problem, whatever you decide.'

Ryan grinned. 'I never thought I'd see the day…' His expression sobered. 'Thanks, Adam. I'll give it some thought.'

Turning back to Hannah, he said, 'I'd better go. I said I would go back to Abby. I'll perhaps see you in a while.'

'That's fine, Ryan. I'll see you later.'

She watched him go, and was glad that his step was jaunty for once. He was getting on with his life and that was good. At the same time, it struck her that she had just witnessed something very special. Adam and Ryan had actually spoken to each other in a warm and friendly way, and just the thought that they were no longer sworn enemies gave her heart a lift. A small glow of hope flickered to life inside her.

Adam was looking at her, his gaze considering. 'That was all a bit of a surprise…though not for you, judging from what you said.'

'I thought there was something going on between them. I'm glad that he's happy at last, and I'm glad for Abby, too. I think they're well suited.'

'That's probably true.' He looked at her. 'It can't have been easy for you, these last few days, standing by and watching as people are reunited with their families…first Dean, and now Abby. It must make you feel disappointed in your own lack of headway.'

'I don't have any choice but to accept it, do I? I've tried everything, and I've gone nowhere, fast.' He had said that he would help with her search, but she wasn't really expecting anything to come of it.

He was silent, then, deep in thought, and she wondered if he had problems of his own. She said tentatively, 'You're very quiet. Is there something on your mind? Did your meeting go as you wanted this morning?'

'It was fine. It went more or less as I expected.'

He didn't say any more, and Hannah was left to wonder whether or not he had been given the job. He seemed relaxed enough, though, despite his contemplative mood, and she guessed that things must have gone his way. It didn't give her any hope for the future.

'Well, perhaps I should get back to work,' she said awkwardly. 'I need to check up on my tachycardia patient.'

He nodded. 'You're off duty tomorrow, aren't you?'

'Yes…why?' Was he thinking of asking her out somewhere? She would go with him in a flash.

'No reason,' he said. 'I was just checking the situation with the duty roster.'

Her hopes were instantly dashed. Why did she keep on hoping that he felt something for her, that he might want her the same way that she wanted him? It wasn't going to happen, was it? Deflated, she went back to work, and tried to put all thoughts of him from her mind.

Back at the flat, she welcomed Abby home and then left her to enjoy her reunion with her parents. They were glad to see their daughter, and it seemed that they were overwhelmed by the prospect of getting to know their grandchild. Abby's mother hugged Ellie, while her husband was busy talking to Ryan and Abby. He looked pleased with the way things were going, and Hannah breathed a sigh of relief that at least Abby's life was changing for the better.

She went into her own sitting room and phoned her mother. 'How are you, Mum?' she asked. 'Is Saxon behaving himself?'

'I'm fine, and, no, he isn't,' her mother said with a chuckle. 'The wretch just chewed up your dad's mobile phone. I swear I'm going to have to take out a bank loan just to cover all the damage he causes. He's a monster mouth on legs.' She laughed, and in the next breath said, 'Have you heard Ryan's good news? He called me earlier today to tell me about his girlfriend, Abby. She sounds like a lovely girl.'

'She is.' Hannah chatted with her for a few minutes, telling her about Abby and Ellie, and how they had managed to find Abby's parents.

'How is your search going?' her mother asked. 'Have you managed to get any closer to finding your real mum?'

'That sounds wrong. You've always been my mum,' Hannah said. 'You know how much I love you, don't you?'

'I do, Hannah…but I know how much it means to you to find out what happened to your birth mother. I do wish that things would go well for you.'

'Adam says he's going to check the hospital records. Perhaps something will turn up.'

She could almost feel her mother's smile. 'I've always liked Adam. I'm sure he'll do his best.'

They talked for a while longer, and then Hannah busied herself with household chores. She felt lost and alone and, more than anything, she wished that Adam could be there with her. With him by her side, everything would be so much brighter.

To her surprise, though, he called for her the next afternoon, just as she was thinking about tackling a pile of ironing. Opening the door to him, she blinked in astonishment. 'I thought you were working today?'

He shook his head. 'I was, but I rearranged the schedules. I want to take you for a drive, to a place in St Albans. Are you up for it?'

'That's where Ryan and I used to live, before we moved house,' she said, puzzled. 'Why are we going there? What's this all about?'

'I'll explain on the way.' He cast a glance over the ironing board and the pile of clothes on the table. 'You didn't really want to stay home and do the ironing, did you? Are you ready? Shall we get started?'

He was all fired up about something, and she was intrigued to know what it was all about. Without giving it any more thought, she grabbed her bag and her jacket and went with him.

CHAPTER TEN

'WHAT's in St Albans?' Hannah asked, as she sat beside Adam in his car and they started to head north.

'I'm hoping that we'll find your mother there…' he said. 'Your natural mother. I did some checking up, and that's where the trail appears to lead. I thought you'd like to see what came of it for yourself.'

She stared at him. 'How can that be? You can't have found an address already, can you?'

He sent her an oblique glance. 'It wasn't easy, because I had to be careful to act within the law, but I did manage to make some headway… And I also had to make sure that I have permission to tell you what I know.'

He was silent for a moment or two as he manoeuvred the car across a junction, but then he added, 'It turns out that your mother was admitted to hospital some eleven years ago, and also on occasion before that. I managed to find out what might have happened to her. She had been ill, on and off, for a long time, as you know, but the diagnosis was always vague and no one could find an explanation for her symptoms. I suppose that's why your father thought she was behaving oddly. He didn't know that there was a medical cause.'

'What was it? What was wrong with her?'

'Her medical team discovered that she had a rare tumour known as a phaeochromocytoma. It was after you went into long-term foster-care, and I think she went into a downward spiral after that. It's probably why she gave you up for adoption, because she must have realised she couldn't cope with looking after a child. The tumour was benign, but it started to produce catecholamines in the adrenal medulla, and that caused her to be hypertensive, and made her emotionally unstable. She suffered weight loss and heart problems, and there were periods of crisis when she would have palpitations, tremor and high blood pressure.'

'All the things that my father put down to alcohol or drugs?'

'I suspect so, but no one knew that she had a tumour at that stage. After all, she'd had a nervous breakdown, and you went into foster-care. It was some time after that, probably when she was living with your grandmother, when the doctors learned the true cause of her troubles. They operated, and gradually she became stronger.'

'But she didn't come back for me.'

'No.' He sent her a quick glance, then turned the car on the road towards St Albans. 'You'll have to ask her the reason for that. All I know is that her medical records were sent from London to St Albans.'

'How do you know that she's my mother? Isn't it possible that this person has the same name?'

'That thought crossed my mind, too. I managed to get hold of an address and phone number, and I took the liberty of ringing her. I didn't want to get your hopes up for no good reason. I spoke to her and when it seemed that I had the right person, I asked if she would agree to see you. She said she wanted to do that and she told me it was all right for me to go through her records and tell you what you needed to know. She hoped that you would understand why you were fostered and put up for adoption.'

Hannah was quiet for a long while. All of this had come as a huge shock to her and now, here she was *en route* to see her mother after all these years. She felt a swift sensation of panic, and she had to struggle to calm herself. How would it be if her mother didn't live up to her expectations...or if her mother was disappointed in her?

It wasn't long before Adam drew the car to a halt in a leafy avenue. It was a quiet residential area, and the houses were all well kept and respectable-looking.

'This is it,' Adam said. 'This is where your mother lives.'

'I don't think I'm ready for this,' Hannah said, her voice faltering. 'I don't think I can go through with it. I need more time.'

'Do you want me to go with you? I will, if that would make it any easier for you. I don't want to intrude on your meeting with her, but I'll stay with you if you want me to do that.'

'Would you?' Her voice was thready, the pulse in her throat hammering as the blood surged in her head. 'I'm nervous. I don't know what to say to her.'

'It'll come. Just keep breathing in deeply, and take things slowly.'

She tried to pull herself together. After a while, when she was feeling up to it, she slid out of the car and stood on the pavement, looking up at the house. She turned to him. 'You won't leave me?'

'I won't.'

Her hand was shaking as she reached up to ring the doorbell, but a woman came and answered the door almost immediately, and they simply stood and stared at each other. The woman was slender, a faded beauty, with a pale face and soft, honey-coloured hair.

'Mum?' Hannah knew her instantly, and it was as though the years melted away in that one moment.

Her mother put her arms out to her. 'Hannah, my angel…you're here at last.'

They held onto each other, and neither of them spoke. It seemed so right to be standing here like this, absorbing comfort from one another, all the hurt forgotten and pushed to one side.

After a long moment, her mother reluctantly released her, and Hannah said in a shaky voice, 'This is Adam. He's very dear to me, and I would like him to stay.'

Her mother nodded. 'Of course. Come in, both of you.' She brushed down her skirt with her fingers and tried to compose herself.

They went into the living room, and sat for a while, and Adam talked quietly to Hannah while her mother went to make coffee for them. It gave Hannah a little time to get herself together.

Then her mother came back into the room and they talked, going over everything that had happened in the intervening years, trying to fill in all the missing pieces of the puzzle.

'I never wanted to give you up for adoption,' her mother said, 'but I was becoming very ill and I knew that I couldn't look after you properly. I'd hoped that your grandmother might be able to help me take care of you, but she was very frail, and I knew that it wouldn't work. I didn't want to mess you about any longer. You'd already suffered when I had the nervous breakdown. I thought it would be better for you if I let you go. I hoped that it would give you the chance to have some stability in your life.'

Hannah thought about that. Then she asked, 'What happened to you after you had the tumour removed? Why didn't you come and find me?'

'I didn't know how to get in touch.' Her mother hesitated, and then offered a plate of biscuits, but Hannah shook her head, refusing them. She was too wound up to eat. She noticed that her mother's arm was not as dexterous as it should have been, and that her grip was awkward. What could have caused that?

'I knew your adoptive mother's original address,' her mother went on, 'but when she moved house, the agency that looked after your records changed. I spoke to the people at the first agency, and they said that the current agency was in a different county. They'd posted all the records over there, but someone messed up and they didn't have any paperwork or anything on computer to say where the files had been sent.'

She frowned. 'I wondered if they were being deliberately vague…after all, it isn't encouraged for parents to contact their children once they've been adopted. I left my name and address in case you wanted to contact me, but soon after that I was taken ill again.'

'Was that after my grandmother died?'

'Yes. I had planned to sell the house and buy a property near to where you originally lived…here in St Albans. I thought if ever you came back here, you might check to see where I was living.' She grimaced. 'It was a long shot, I know. Of course, by then I had married again, and my name had changed. Perhaps that was what caused some of the mix-up. It has all been such a mess.'

Hannah frowned. It hadn't occurred to her for quite a while to go back to the area where she had once lived. By the time she had done that, her mother must have started using her married name.

'You said that you were taken ill again… What happened? Did the tumour come back?'

Her mother shook her head. 'No, but I still suffered from occasional bouts of hypertension before they could get my medication right, and I had a stroke. It turned out that there was a vascular malformation in my head, and the blood vessel ruptured. I was lucky that my neighbours saw me collapse and called an ambulance right away. I think if they had delayed, I might not have survived. As it was, it took me a long time to recover from the paralysis.'

Hannah closed her eyes briefly, trying to take in all that had been said. Adam spoke softly to her mother, saying, 'You've been through too much, and it seems as though you've had a raw deal. How are you now? Is everything under control?'

'Yes, I believe it is. I have regular medical supervision, and my husband is a good man. We met when I was recovering from the stroke. He's seen me through a lot, and he takes care of me. He's kept me going through all the bad times. I wanted to get in touch with Hannah and it hurt so much when I couldn't find her. I suppose she must have been working in different places all the time that she was doing her medical training, but I didn't know where to start to look. Then I thought that perhaps she wouldn't thank me for disturbing her life all over again. She had such a disrupted childhood, one way and another.'

'I'm glad that I've found you at last,' Hannah said. 'I don't ever want to lose you again.'

They stayed with her mother for a long time, talking things through, remembering all that had gone on in the past.

It was late evening when Hannah said reluctantly, 'I think it's time we started back to London. I have to work in the morning.' She gave her mother a hug, and said, 'Will you keep in touch? Will you come over to my adoptive mother's house some time? I'll probably be staying there for a while when my stint at the hospital finishes.'

'You won't be able to keep me away.'

A short time later, after they had exchanged addresses and phone numbers, Adam drove Hannah back to London. Instead of taking her back to her flat, though, he parked the car at his Bayswater apartment. 'I thought you could do with some time to yourself,' he said. 'All this has come as a bit of a shock to you, hasn't it? Back at your flat, you'll probably have to start explaining things to Abby and Ryan, and even to Dean, and at least here you can have a bit of a breathing space.'

She smiled. 'That's true.' She gazed up at him as they walked into his living room a few minutes later. 'I don't know how to begin to thank you for what you've done. I've waited so long for this day, and yet, now that it's finally arrived, I'm overwhelmed by all that's happened.'

'That's understandable.'

She said softly, 'I want to ring my mum, and let her know what's happened.'

He nodded. 'I'll give you some space while you do that. I'll make some food for us. It won't be anything special, perhaps a pizza and salad—would that be all right?'

'That will be lovely, thanks.' She hadn't realised how hungry she was. All the time she had been with her real mother, she had been keyed up, on edge, and now she was finally beginning to come down to earth once more.

Her adoptive mother was thrilled to hear her news. 'I'm so glad for you, Hannah,' she said. 'It must be wonderful for you to have found her after all this time. Would she come and visit with us, do you think? I could make room for her and her husband to stay with us for a while, if you like. It might be a bit of a squeeze, but we'll cope somehow.'

'That's what I love about you,' Hannah said, a smile

in her voice. 'You're always there for me. You make everything right. I'm sure she would love to come and stay. I'll ask her.'

They talked for a little while longer, and then Adam appeared with the food, and Hannah said goodbye and promised to come home soon.

'She's invited my mother and her husband to stay over for a few days,' she told him. 'Isn't that thoughtful of her?'

'You always knew she had a good heart,' Adam said. He placed a tray of food on the table in front of them and sat beside her. 'Tuck in. You must be starving by now.'

'I am.' She tasted the pizza, letting the cheese dissolve slowly on her tongue. 'This is delicious,' she told him. 'It's the best food I've ever tasted.'

'Hmm…that's what finding your mother does for you.' He watched her eat, his expression absorbed, and she looked at him curiously.

'What are you thinking?'

'That I'm glad that you're happy. I've wanted you to feel this way for a long time, but it makes me wary of asking what I want to ask.'

She finished her pizza and licked her fingers clean, looking at him in bewilderment. 'You can ask me anything you want. Why would you hold back? I owe you so much.'

'You don't owe me anything at all.' He was quiet for a moment, and then said, 'Are you really set on going back home when this stint in A and E comes to an end? Have you thought about working as a general practitioner in London?'

'I'm not sure that I could do that,' she said cautiously. 'I think I would miss my family back home. I've always planned on working in a rural community.' She looked at him, her gaze searching his face. 'Why are you suggesting it?' A faint glow of hope was sparking to life inside her. Did he want her to stay? Wouldn't she be able to find it in herself to do that for him?

'I was hoping that we could find a way to be together,' he said. 'I know it's a lot to ask, but I always knew that you would never be able to settle until you found your real mother, and I know that this is the wrong time to talk about it when you're still getting used to the idea that she's close by. I'm just afraid that time's running out, and we'll soon be going our separate ways, and I really don't want that to happen.'

'You don't?' She looked into his eyes and tried to see what he was keeping from her. 'You never said anything before about wanting me to stay on.'

His mouth made a rueful shape. 'I thought there was something going on between you and Ryan. I kept trying to get close to you and always something came between us. I could understand that you were taken up with wanting to find your mother, but at the back of my mind I thought perhaps you were in love with Ryan. I wanted to tell you that I'm the one who loves you, and that I can make you happy if only you'll let me, but I could see how close you were to him and I was afraid that you might care for him more than you did for me.'

She pulled in a sharp breath. Was he really saying that he loved her? 'How could you think that way?' she said. 'Ryan is like a brother to me. We've always been like brother and sister.'

'I didn't see it that way. You aren't related by blood, and there's such a strong bond between the two of you that I felt like an intruder. I love you, but I didn't want to make you choose between us.'

She reached out and touched him, her fingers cupping his cheek. 'You had it all wrong,' she said. 'I've come to realise over these last few months just how much I care for you. I love you, Adam. I think I've always loved you, but things got in the way, and we seemed to lead such different lives. I didn't believe it would ever be possible for us to be together.'

His arms closed around her. 'I've loved you for as long as I can remember. I couldn't make a move because I knew that you weren't ready. You were young and insecure, and even though I wanted to bring you with me when I left my father's estate, it didn't feel right to drag you away from your safe haven. I was glad when you turned up here in London. I knew that you had made the move of your own accord and I thought there might at least be some hope for us.'

He leaned towards her and kissed her then, his mouth pressuring hers, tasting the fullness of her lips, his arms circling her as though he would never let her go. 'I want you so much,' he murmured against her cheek. 'I need you, Hannah. I want you to stay with me and be mine.'

She kissed him in return, her hands reaching up and curving around his neck, bringing his head closer to hers and leaving a trail of kisses along his cheekbone, his jaw line, his mouth. 'I thought you would never ask,' she whispered.

His hands moved over her, shaping her curves, exploring the soft silk of her skin. 'You're all I've ever wanted,' he said in a roughened voice. 'I didn't know how I was going to live without you.'

She curled up against him. 'What are we going to do? I don't know if I can cope with living in the city. I never had it in mind to stay.'

'Then I'll have to find work near to where you want to be. Don't worry about it. We'll work something out.'

'Will we?' She looked up at him. 'What about the job at the hospital? I thought it was yours already?'

'It's mine if I want it, but I've been looking into other options, nearer home, just in case you should decide to go back there.'

'You wouldn't mind doing that? You always seemed to love being here in London. What about this fabulous apartment, the excitement and opportunity of working in London? Isn't that what you've always wanted?'

'I thought that was what I wanted, but one city is much like another, and I'll find a consultant post close to where you want to be. I already have a place in mind.' His gaze moved over her. 'Home is wherever you are, Hannah. I want you to be happy—that's more important to me than anything else.'

He kissed her gently, savouring the moment. 'Will you marry me, Hannah? Will you be my wife?'

Her breath caught in her throat. 'Oh, yes, Adam. Yes…'

He smiled into her eyes. 'You've just made me the happiest man in the world.' His fingers slid over her face, and along the column of her throat, his lips following in their wake, trailing kisses along the creamy expanse of her shoulder, nudging aside the flimsy cotton top she was wearing.

She moved closer to him, or maybe he urged her to him, she wasn't sure how it came about, but the softness of her breasts was crushed against his hard male frame, and his hands explored her, his palm cupping the swell of her breast. Desire surged inside her, causing her mind to dissolve into cotton-wool cloudiness, and her body began to tremble with need.

'I want you,' she whispered. 'I want to be with you, to know that you're always going to be here with me.'

'Then that's how it will be,' he said raggedly against her mouth. 'We'll find a fabulous house in the country, and make it ours.'

Her eyes widened. 'A place like this, with a roof terrace and a terrific view over the surrounding country-side?'

'Whatever you want. You only have to say and it's yours.'

She smiled up at him. 'I was just kidding,' she said softly. 'I just want to be wherever you are.'

'Me, too.' He kissed her again, with infinite tenderness that swiftly yielded to burning passion. 'I love you, Hannah.'

'I love you,' she whispered, and kissed him again, settling into his heated embrace, her head resting in the crook of his shoulder.

He looked into her eyes, and now she could at last read what he was thinking. His gaze told her all that she wanted to know. It said that they would be as one, like this, for all time. Then he lowered his head and claimed her mouth, and she forgot everything for a long, long while as she gave herself up to the promise of that kiss.

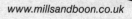

4 FREE

BOOKS AND A SURPRISE GIFT!

We would like to take this opportunity to thank you for reading this Mills & Boon® book by offering you the chance to take FOUR more specially selected titles from the Medical Romance™ series absolutely FREE! We're also making this offer to introduce you to the benefits of the Reader Service™—

- ★ FREE home delivery
- ★ FREE gifts and competitions
- ★ FREE monthly Newsletter
- ★ Exclusive Reader Service offers
- ★ Books available before they're in the shops

Accepting these FREE books and gift places you under no obligation to buy, you may cancel at any time, even after receiving your free shipment. Simply complete your details below and return the entire page to the address below. You don't even need a stamp!

YES! Please send me 4 free Medical Romance books and a surprise gift. I understand that unless you hear from me, I will receive 6 superb new titles every month for just £2.80 each, postage and packing free. I am under no obligation to purchase any books and may cancel my subscription at any time. The free books and gift will be mine to keep in any case.

M6ZED

Ms/Mrs/Miss/Mr ....Initials ....

BLOCK CAPITALS PLEASE

Surname ....

Address ....

....

....Postcode..

Send this whole page to:
UK: FREEPOST CN81, Croydon, CR9 3WZ